PAPER WISHES

PAPER WISHES

Lois Sepahban

SQUARE
FISH
Margaret Ferguson Books
Farrar Straus Giroux
New York

Thanks to Carrie Andresen-Strawn of the Manzanar National Historic Site
for her careful reading and suggestions.

SQUARE
FISH

An imprint of Macmillan Publishing Group, LLC
175 Fifth Avenue
New York, NY 10010
mackids.com

Our books may be purchased in bulk for promotional, educational, or business use. Please
contact your local bookseller or the Macmillan Corporate and Premium Sales Department
at (800) 221-7945 ext. 5442 or by e-mail at MacmillanSpecialMarkets@macmillan.com.

Library of Congress Cataloging-in-Publication Data
Sepahban, Lois.
    Paper wishes / Lois Sepahban.
      pages cm
    Summary: Near the start of World War II, young Manami, her parents,
and Grandfather are evacuated from their home and sent to Manzanar, an ugly,
dreary internment camp in the desert for Japanese-American citizens.
    ISBN 978-1-250-10414-4 (paperback)   ISBN 978-0-374-30217-7 (ebook)
    1. Japanese Americans—Evacuation and relocation, 1942–1945—Juvenile
fiction. [1. Japanese Americans—Evacuation and relocation, 1942–1945—Fiction.
2. Manzanar War Relocation Center—Fiction. 3. Mutism—Fiction.
4. Family life—Fiction. 5. World War, 1939–1945—United States—Fiction.]
I. Title.

PZ7.1.S462Pap 2016
[Fic]—dc23

                                                              2015005786

Originally published in the United States by Farrar Straus Giroux
First Square Fish Edition: 2017
Book designed by Roberta Pressel
Square Fish logo designed by Filomena Tuosto

10   9   8

AR: 3.8 / LEXILE: 550L

For Amir, Bella, and Julian,
with all of my love,
and for Strider,
who would have found a way
if there had been one

MARCH

Grandfather says that a man should walk barefoot on the bare earth every day. Mother says that a man can do so if he likes, but her daughter will wear shoes. I explain this to Grandfather when he tells me to take off my shoes.

We are sitting on our special rock at the beach where the soil ends and the sand begins.

Grandfather laughs.

"Manami," he says, "there was a time when my daughter did not always wear shoes either. My daughter is correct: you should wear shoes. But we are going to walk on the beach. So for now, take them off. Otherwise they will fill with sand and salt water. My daughter would not like your shoes to be ruined."

I know he is right, so I take off my shoes and follow Grandfather to the dark, wet sand where the beach ends and the water begins.

As the water splashes my feet, I stop and curl my toes into the sand until it buries my ankles. The salt spray smells of seaweed and fish. Grandfather walks along the shore away from me, his slow, steady steps leaving a footprint path. I watch the tide rush up to meet him. When it pulls away, his footprints are gone. It's as if he was never there. For a moment, I feel uneasy, like yesterday when soldiers arrived. But then I spy Yujiin racing toward me and I forget Grandfather's footprints. Yujiin must have escaped through the window again.

Yujiin is not a puppy—he has not been a puppy for a very long time. But he races and he jumps and he yaps at me, his white fur flecked with dried bits of sand. I scoop him up and run to Grandfather. Yujiin struggles to be free of my arms, even more eager than I am to be by Grandfather's side. I set Yujiin down next to Grandfather's feet.

When he is with Grandfather, Yujiin behaves like an old man. He does not race or jump or yap. Like Grandfather, he walks slowly. But Yujiin is so small that he leaves no footprints to wash away. Only smears of sand that are invisible unless you look carefully. When he hears a sound Yujiin cocks his head and looks Grandfather in the eye.

Grandfather nods at Yujiin and tells him that he has heard the strange sound, too. I remind Grandfather that ships' horns are not strange at all. I remind him that this is Bainbridge Island and the port is only a mile away. I remind him that ships come to our island every day.

"That is so," Grandfather says. "But this ship is different. It is a warship. Warships do not come to our port every day."

I feel uneasy again, and I take Grandfather's hand in mine.

"Why have the soldiers come?" I ask.

"War," Grandfather says. "It means soldiers everywhere."

"When I see the soldiers, I am scared," I say.

"When the soldiers see you, they are scared, too," Grandfather says.

"Me?" I ask. I do not think I look scary.

"You. Me. All of us. They think: Maybe these people with Japanese faces and Japanese names will betray us," Grandfather says.

"But only my face and my name are Japanese," I say. "The rest of me is American."

"That is so," Grandfather says.

We step away from the water's edge and return to our rock.

Grandfather sits on it. Yujiin perches next to him. I sit beside them.

"Look at the ocean," Grandfather says. "Where does it end? Where does it begin?"

"It ends when you reach the mainland," I tell him. "It begins right here."

"Perhaps," Grandfather says.

We watch the waves roll in and out.

We hear them crash against the shore.

I match my breath to the tide, in and out, calming my nervous stomach.

Yujiin licks my hand. Then he licks Grandfather's hand.

"I remember, dear friend," Grandfather says to Yujiin, "that it was in this very spot that we first met. I, alone and grieving. You, alone and hungry."

This is a story I know well.

An old story.

It happened just after Grandmother died.

"You have school. It is time for us to go," Grandfather says. His voice is soft and sad. Yujiin cocks his head at me and looks in my eye. I pick him up and whisper in his ear: I hear Grandfather's sadness, too.

The bell is ringing when Grandfather and Yujiin and I arrive at the school yard. I kiss Grandfather's cheek and run to join my classmates.

"Bye!" I shout over my shoulder.

Mother does not think I should shout.

"Bye!" he shouts back.

But Grandfather does not mind.

"Manami!" My friend Kimmi waves for me to join her.

When I reach her, we link arms and she whispers in my ear.

"Soldiers!" she says.

"I know!" I say.

"My mother thinks they will send us all to prison!" Kimmi says.

Ryo pushes his face close to us. "My father thinks they will send us all to Japan!" he says.

I do not like Ryo. Or his pushing. But Kimmi's mother is kind.

I wonder: Are the soldiers here to take us away?

"Come along, children," Mrs. Brown calls.

We follow her into the school building.

Through the hallway.

Into our classroom.

My heart is beating quickly after what Kimmi and Ryo said.

I sink into my seat next to Kimmi.

Mrs. Brown looks at us. She clears her throat.

I think she is going to say something important.

But then she says, "Sarah Beth, it is your turn to recite."

Sarah Beth stands and recites a poem.

Just another school day. Another Tuesday. Like last week and all the weeks before.

But at the end of school Mrs. Brown asks me and Kimmi and Ryo and a few others to stay in the classroom.

Our classmates send us secret looks as they put on their coats and leave.

"Children," Mrs. Brown says, "this is to be your last school day. Your parents will explain. Gather your things now."

I think: Mrs. Brown does not know my parents very well. They do not explain anything. Not even about the soldiers who came yesterday.

"Children," Mrs. Brown says when we are ready to leave. Her voice is shaky. "This is not your fault. Remember, this is not your fault. I will miss you. And I will pray that I see you again soon."

I run home.

Mother's forehead is wrinkled in a frown, her sewing in her hands. Father's back is hunched over rope and fishing lines. Grandfather and Yujiin are not there. They must be at the beach.

"There are posters," I say. "All over town."

My parents look at each other.

"The posters say *Evacuate*," I tell them.

"We have seen the posters," Father says. He is still looking at Mother.

After a moment, they continue their work.

I feel tears burn my eyes.

"Mrs. Brown said I cannot go back to school."

My parents look at me.

Mother hurries to my side and holds my hand. Father reaches across the table to wipe my tears.

"Why?" I ask.

I wait for my parents to explain.

But I am right: my parents do not explain anything.

Instead, they say, "Do not worry."

Early the next morning, Grandfather takes me and Yujiin to the beach. We walk and walk and walk. But we do not talk. Normal and not normal.

When we return home, the door to our small house is open, delicious smells wafting outside. Normal and not normal.

Inside, Mother and Grandfather share a long look. Normal and not normal.

Father is sitting at the kitchen table. Normal and not normal.

Normal would be: Grandfather and me talking on our walk.

Normal would be: delicious smells of broth and fruit, not stew and brined fish.

Normal would be: Mother and Grandfather sharing a long smile.

Normal would be: Father in a fishing boat at this time of day. Or Father at the table, but later, in the evening.

I pretend everything is normal and go to my room. Once, I shared my room with my sister, Keiko, and my brother, Ron. They are far away now, in Indiana. They go to school at Earlham College. Their beds are still here, in case they visit. They do visit sometimes. But my brother will not be a fisherman like Father, and my sister will not marry a fisherman like Mother did.

There is clear, icy water in my wash basin. I splash my face and neck and rub my skin with a towel. When I am red and shiny, I leave my room to join my family for breakfast.

Yujiin has not left Grandfather's side. He is curled up under Grandfather's chair, but not at rest. His head is up, his eyes are sharp, his ears are alert.

Mother stirs the stew pot.

Father makes a list.

Grandfather scratches Yujiin's head.

I scoop tea leaves into a pot and pour boiling water over them. I take the teapot and four cups to the table.

I ladle rice into a large bowl. I take the bowl and four plates to the table.

I arrange fruit on a platter. I take the platter to the table.

When I sit down, Mother is still stirring, Father is still writing, and Grandfather is still scratching Yujiin.

"Something is wrong," I say.

"Nothing is wrong, little one," says Grandfather. "We are all here. Together."

"I can feel that something is wrong," I insist.

"Everything is fine, Daughter," says Father. "Have your tea."

"Mother?" I ask.

"All will be well," she says.

I look at Yujiin and he looks at me. He knows something is wrong, too.

For the first time in my life, I wish it was a school day. Then I remember. It is a school day. Just not for me.

After breakfast, Mother sends me to my room to change into my blue gardening dress.

Outside, I pull every single weed.

Mother inspects the garden and hands me a basket. "Harvest all that you can," she says.

"There is nothing to harvest," I tell her, which she knows better than I do. There will be nothing for at least two months.

"All the herbs," she says. "Gather them and wrap them in cloth. Dig up the garlic and onions. Put them in a pillowcase with dirt."

I cut down herbs, their green juice soaking into the soil. I wrap them and pack them, just as Mother says. I rake up garlic bulbs and onions that are too small for even one person, leaving broken mounds and dirt clods in my wake.

When I finish, Mother calls me inside for lunch—fish stew.

Then she has more work for me.

We wash shirts and skirts and dresses and pants.

We fold towels and sheets.

Mother lays out envelopes of seeds on the table. "Throw out empty envelopes. Stack everything else here," she says.

I am tired of this work. I want to ask, "Why so much work?" But I don't.

We stop again for dinner—more fish stew.

"Off to bed," Mother tells me.

"But—" I start to say.

"Please, Manami," Father says.

In my bedroom, I try to hear what Mother and Father and Grandfather are talking about. But I cannot. Ron's dictionary catches my eye, and I look up a word.

Evacuate: to leave a place, a dangerous place or a military zone.

That word rolls around inside my head: *evacuate, evacuate, evacuate.*

After a while, I am too tired to think or worry. My shoulders and arms ache, but I sleep well.

When I come into the kitchen the next day, I find Mother sitting at the table alone. She motions for me to eat.

She combs my hair in long, strong strokes and twists it into two tight braids.

"Something is wrong," I tell her.

"Yes."

I wait, but she doesn't say more.

I have been patient. But I can't be patient anymore.

"Tell me."

"We must leave in four days," she says after a moment.

Evacuate: to leave a place.

"Why?"

"I do not know," she says.

"Where will we go?"

"I do not know."

"For how long?"

"I do not know."

These are not good answers.

I wait, but these are the only answers I get.

"We have to go into town today to register and have a medical examination," Mother says.

"But I am not sick."

"Everyone must be checked."

Father and Grandfather and Mother and I walk into town.

We pass many buildings: the courthouse, the police station, churches, the library.

When we pass the school, I twist my neck to try to see inside the window of my classroom. My classmates' heads are bent over their desks. I wonder what they are reading.

Others are walking into town, too.

Others with dark hair and dark eyes.

Others like us.

It is easy to see where we should report. Even without the soldiers and their guns. The sidewalk is so crowded that people line one side of the street and wrap around the corner.

Ahead of me, Father and Grandfather join the line.

Mother tugs my hand. "Quickly," she says.

I see Kimmi sitting on the post office steps.

"Can I play over there with Kimmi?" I ask.

"Families must stay together," Mother says.

An hour later, we are still in line. Still on the sidewalk. But at least we have reached a table where a soldier is seated.

"Name?" the soldier asks.

"Tanaka," Father says, pointing to himself and Mother and me.

"Ishii," Grandfather says.

"We are together," Father says.

"Your family number is 104313," the soldier says. He hands Father paper tags with strings attached to them. "Place these on all of your luggage. Each family member must wear a tag, too. Maybe tie it to your coats."

Father gives the tags to Mother and she puts them in her purse.

"Move to that line," the soldier says, pointing. "After your medical exams, you'll be done. Be ready for transportation early Monday morning."

Inside the building, we are shown to a large room.

We sit for a long time on cots.

"This is worse than standing!" I say.

"Don't fidget," Mother says.

Finally a doctor comes.

Healthy.

Healthy.

Healthy.

Healthy.

I could have told him that.

Then we walk home.

Mother sets an open suitcase on my bed.

"Let's see what fits," she says.

We fold and pack all of my clothes: four dresses, two pairs of pants, two nightgowns, four shirts, my coat, underclothes, and shoes.

The suitcase doesn't close.

"Sit on top," Mother says.

With me sitting on it, Mother is able to snap it shut.

"We can't take it all," she says. "You can wear your coat. But we still have to fit sheets and a blanket and dishes."

"We need another suitcase," I say.

"We cannot carry another," she says.

We empty my suitcase and set it next to the other open suitcases.

I watch Mother fit things inside like pieces of a puzzle: dishes, bedding, clothes, seed envelopes, the bag of onions and garlic, a photograph of Grandmother, Father's small box with fishing gear and tools, Grandfather's tiny sand rake, Mother's gardening tools.

The pieces do not fit.

"Go play," Mother says. Then she begins unpacking the suitcases again.

The day before we are to leave, I find Mother sitting at the table. She is wearing her best dress and hat. She is wearing stockings, which I did not know she had, and high heels, which I have secretly worn myself. She is wearing lipstick, bright red. I want to wipe it off, to see if, underneath the red, Mother is still there.

She looks at me with sad eyes. "Put on your best dress," she tells me. "Today, we say goodbye to our friends."

Grandfather and Father and Mother and I go to the church. Pastor Rob holds a special service. All of our friends are there. Our Japanese friends, like Mr. Matsuo, who grows the best strawberries. Our American friends, like my teacher, Mrs. Brown. And our friends who are like me and Kimmi. Japanese and American. Both at the same time. Or maybe neither one.

Our American friends cry after the service.

"This will be over soon," they tell us.

Early the next morning, early before I am ready, Mother wakes me.

I get up and see the four suitcases by the door. Three are closed. One is open.

While I put on my clothes, Mother takes my nightgown, folds it neatly into the open suitcase, and shuts it.

We eat breakfast without speaking.

We eat breakfast in a hurry.

"It is time," Father says.

Grandfather fills a bowl with water and a bowl with rice. He sets them on Yujiin's food mat. He picks up Yujiin and holds him against his face. He puts Yujiin on the ground near his mat.

"Pastor Rob will come for you later this morning," he says. "Goodbye, dear friend."

Then Grandfather picks up his suitcase and walks out the door.

"Mother!" I say.

Tears run down her cheeks. She picks up her suitcase and follows Grandfather.

"Father?"

He picks up his suitcase and waits for me outside.

I want to shout. I want to kick and scream at them. Instead, I whisper, "Yujiin!"

He jumps into my arms, and I hide him under my coat.

"Down!" I tell him.

He crouches low in my arm.

I lift my suitcase, go outside, and watch Father lock the door. Then we join Mother and Grandfather at the side of the road.

A truck stops in front of us.

An army truck.

Soldiers jump out and pick up our suitcases. They help Mother and Grandfather into the back. Father joins them, and I hurry behind him before anyone tries to help me.

Others are there in the truck.

Neighbors.

Friends.

People with Japanese faces and Japanese names.

Just like me.

Two soldiers sit in the back of the truck, too.

I squeeze into a corner.

The truck is noisy and everyone has worried eyes.

That is good because they don't notice me and Yujiin.

It doesn't take long to drive to the port.

When I step out of the truck, there are people everywhere. Walking, sitting, rushing, waiting. And so much noise. Talking, shouting, stomping, honking. I see Pastor Rob. Arms wave goodbye. Hands wipe tears from cheeks.

"Stay near," Mother tells me.

"Each person may only bring what they can carry!" a voice shouts above the crowd.

Father has tied our number tags on our suitcases. We join a long line.

Mother holds Grandfather's arm. At the front of the line there is commotion. A child has wandered off. A suitcase has burst open. Suddenly, it is our turn.

"104313," Father says, and points to the tags we are wearing. He speaks loudly. His shoulders are back and his head is high.

A baby starts to fuss behind us.

Yujiin whines. I pinch his leg. I am afraid Grandfather will hear him.

"Leave your suitcases there," the soldier says. He points to me and starts to say something, but then the baby screams. The soldier shakes his head and waves us toward the ferryboat.

I am grateful for the screaming baby.

Father and Mother and Grandfather take seats on the lower deck. I pretend to need fresh air so that Mother will let me stand a few steps away near the rail.

When I peek inside my coat, Yujiin stares up at me. He is panting, and I know he is hot. But I do not dare take him out. I try to angle my coat to let cool air blow inside.

The boat begins our journey, and the island shrinks smaller and smaller until it has disappeared in fog. If I cannot see the island, is it still there?

I watch for the mainland. It grows out of nothing, bigger and bigger until it is all that I can see.

Such a short trip. Less than an hour.

But such a long trip, too. Far from home.

Mother calls to me. I pull my coat close over Yujiin again and return to my family. As soon as she sees me, Mother fusses with my hair, my cheeks, my collar. Her eyes go to my arm that is clutched against my side.

"What is under your coat?" she asks.

Yujiin pokes his nose through the opening between two buttons of my coat.

"Manami, what have you done?"

"Mother," I say, "I could not leave Yujiin."

"Shh," she says. "We will hope."

I see Grandfather watching us, a frown on his brow. Mother catches my eye and shakes her head.

When we get off the ferry, we do not have to wait so long in line as before. The soldiers who accompanied us on the boat lead us to buses that will take us to a passenger train. A new soldier stands next to the bus, checking numbers as people board. Mother holds me close to her, Yujiin squeezed between us.

The new soldier motions for us to board the bus. As we walk past him, his eyes linger on me. On my arm. On Mother's arm.

"Wait!" he shouts. Everyone freezes. Father, Grandfather, Mother. Even the other people in line.

"What are you hiding?" he asks me.

Father looks at me and then at Mother.

I look down. I press my lips closed.

"Girl!" the soldier says. "What is under your coat?"

Mother unbuttons my coat, revealing Yujiin sitting on my forearm, pressed against my side.

I look up.

"Manami!" Father says. "No!"

Mother is crying.

"No dogs!" the soldier says. He points to a crate.

I will not put Yujiin in that crate.

Mother covers her face with her hands. Father's face turns red.

Grandfather stares at me. He takes Yujiin and puts him in the crate. When he stands again, his shoulders sag and tears run down his cheeks.

This time, I shout. I kick and scream.

APRIL

For two days, we ride on a train. I remember very little of the first day.

Yujiin, his nose pushing through a gap in the crate.

Father, his arms holding me to his chest.

Mother, her hand resting on Grandfather's shoulder.

But that is all.

Now I keep still so that no one will notice that I am awake.

Father sits next to me, his head resting against the back of the seat, his eyes closed.

Mother sits across from Father, also sleeping.

Grandfather stares at a blind that covers a window.

Across the aisle, others sleep. Ryo, though, peeks behind a corner of the blind covering his window.

A soldier walks toward him, his boots heavy even over the loud rumble and clack of the train. Mother wakes and leans forward to tap Father's knee. Others wake up, too.

When Ryo sees the soldier, he drops the edge of the blind.

"Good morning," the soldier says. He lifts the blind and moves to the next window, raising blinds one after the other.

Another soldier brings a cart loaded with boxes of food.

"Breakfast!" he calls.

The soldiers sit among my neighbors, eating and talking with them. My neighbors do not look afraid of the soldiers. And the soldiers do not look afraid of us.

Father sits near the soldiers, eating and talking.

Mother brings a box with fruit and bread. She offers it to Grandfather.

"No, Daughter," he says.

Kimmi sits on Father's seat.

She leans close to me and whispers, "I'm sorry about Yujiin."

I do not want to think about this.

I close my eyes and pretend to fall asleep.

Maybe I do sleep.

When I open my eyes, the breakfast cart is gone. Kimmi is gone. Father is gone. Mother is still here, her hand on Grandfather's shoulder again.

"So ugly," I hear someone say.

"So empty," I hear someone else say. "Where are the trees?"

"I hope we don't end up someplace like that," another voice adds.

The train slows to a stop.

We step off the train and board the waiting buses. The buses will drive us to our destination.

As we get closer, I see bits and pieces through my window.

Fence.

Barbed wire.

Guard tower.

Buildings covered with black paper.

Red dirt.

I read the sign: *Manzanar.*

It is ugly.

And we do end up in this place.

The soldiers help us off the buses and motion to us to gather in a group while our luggage is unloaded. I see that there are many people I don't recognize. I do not know where they have come from.

While we wait for instructions, Mother says, "Desert. There's no water. No green."

Her cheeks are wet with tears.

"It is a prison," she says.

"The soldiers say it will be a village," Father says. "We will make it a village."

. . .

A soldier calls out numbers from a paper.

The island families follow the soldier.

"Block 1!" the soldier shouts, pointing to the right, to rows of black-covered buildings.

"Administration!" he shouts, pointing to the left.

We walk past the buildings and then cross a dirt road.

"Block 2!" he shouts, pointing to the right at more black-covered buildings.

"Garage!" he shouts, pointing to the left.

We cross another dirt road.

"Block 3!" he shouts, pointing to the right. "Your block."

Block 3 looks like the other blocks: black-covered buildings lined up in two rows. But the buildings in Block 3 are not all finished.

This is where the island families will live.

"There are fourteen barracks per block," the soldier says. "Each barracks will be divided into four rooms."

The soldier taps a building and says, "Barracks 1." He calls out numbers and tells each family which room is theirs.

He goes to Barracks 2 and then Barracks 3. At Barracks 4, he calls our number.

"That's us," Father says.

I touch the black wall of the building before I go inside. It is rough and almost sticky.

We go to our room, and another island family comes inside, too. The Soto family. I count. There are ten people in here. But there are only eight cots.

Mother walks to the back corner and arranges four cots into a rectangle.

Father and Mr. Soto go outside.

Grandfather sits on a cot. "I have lived too long," he says.

My heart squeezes when I hear Grandfather's words.

Mother rushes to him and holds his hands. "All will be well," she says.

The other children sit in a heap on the floor.

Mother helps Mrs. Soto arrange suitcases and cots. Mrs. Soto has a large belly and a baby coming at any moment.

"Sit," Mother tells her. "You need to rest."

Mrs. Soto starts to cry.

I curl up into a ball on the cot next to Grandfather's.

Mother nails a string from one wall to the wall across from it. Then she drapes sheets over the string.

"Now we have more privacy," she says.

I look around. Inside our room I can hear the whispers of the Soto family. I can smell many bodies in one small space. There is no privacy, I think.

Loud clanging makes the Soto children freeze. The clanging continues, and they start to cry. Mrs. Soto hushes them. Mother goes outside to see what is happening.

"Time for dinner," she says when she returns. "You must bring your own dishes."

After Mrs. Soto and her children leave, Mother takes my hand.

"Come, Manami," she says, pulling me to my feet.

I don't let go of her hand.

"Father?" Mother asks.

"I'm not hungry," says Grandfather.

"I'll bring something back for you," Mother says.

Mother and I carry our dishes and join our neighbors outside. A line winds past the black-covered barracks to a larger building. It seems as if everyone in Block 3 is here.

"Manami!" Kimmi is ahead of us, waving her hand. She skips down the line to stand with us.

"Our barracks is crowded," she says. "I am in number 7. What number are you in?"

Mother answers Kimmi. "Number 4," she says. "Who is in your barracks?"

I can hear Kimmi and Mother talking, but I do not pay attention.

Then Kimmi squeezes my hand. "See you soon," she says before she goes back to her mother.

Father joins Mother and me in the slow-moving line. A sign near the door says *Mess Hall Block 3*.

The mess hall is filled with tables and benches. The line moves toward the back, where food is being served. There is a long table. Three people stand behind it, scooping food onto our dishes. I collect my dinner and follow Mother and Father to an empty spot at a table. The room rumbles with low voices and forks clinking against plates.

I am hungry, so I take a bite of the mashed potatoes on my plate.

They are sticky and thick, and the more I try to swallow, the stickier and thicker they grow. I do not like these potatoes.

But I am still hungry, so I take a bite of the corn on my plate.

It has no flavor. But at least it isn't sticky and thick.

There is some kind of meat, too. It is shaped like a square.

I try to imagine a bowl of rice and a plate of fruit.

I am hungry, so I eat the food. But I do not like it.

I soon discover that if I crouch down low with my eyes next to the ground, I can pretend that the dirt looks like sand here.

If I stand tall with my feet bare, I can pretend the dirt feels like sand here.

But when I open my mouth to speak, the dirt no longer feels like sand. It sticks to my lips and tongue like red mud. It coats my throat so that I cannot speak.

I think this is what has happened to me.

I wish the dirt would cloud my eyes, too, so that I would not see this place that is and is not my home without Yujiin.

"Say something," Mother tells me. We have been here two days and she is sitting behind me on my bed, her arms wrapped around me and her mouth next to my ear.

It feels good to sit like this.

"You are sad," she says. "Maybe even angry."

I close my eyes and listen to her words. Sad and angry, yes, maybe. But mostly scared and worried.

"Go outside and play with the other children," she says.

Before the door closes behind me, I hear Grandfather speak.

"Let her be," he says.

"But she won't talk," Mother says.

"Give her time," he says.

Kimmi waves to me from the big open space between Block 2 and Block 3.

Many children play there.

They talk and laugh.

Some play with marbles.

Some play with a ball.

Some stand in groups giggling.

Kimmi asks me a question, but I cannot answer.

"It's okay," Kimmi says. "I know you're sad. I miss Yu-jiin, too."

"What's wrong with her?" someone asks.

"Leave her alone!" Kimmi says.

"Why won't she talk?"

"Just leave her alone!" Kimmi says again.

Kimmi holds my hand tighter.

But I don't want to be in this place with these children.

I step backward. Kimmi looks at me and then lets my hand go.

"See you later," she whispers.

Father starts to join the other fathers in the morning. They work all day, clearing brush for new buildings, and some help finish the barracks in Block 3. Each is just like ours. A long rectangle, divided into four rooms. They will keep building new blocks filled with more barracks, thirty-six blocks in all.

After two weeks, Father gets permission for us to move to a new barracks in Block 3.

"Barracks 8 is finished now," Father explains.

We carry our suitcases to the room Father tells us is our new home.

Inside, it is the same as the room in Barracks 4.

Sharp scent of fresh wood.

A window where dust can blow in because there are gaps in the frame.

Mother empties the pillowcase of dirt and garlic and onions onto the ground outside. She washes the pillowcase and cuts the seams. She sews the edges, making a curtain. She nails it over the window.

Light filters in, but dirt mostly stays out.

Outside, along the wall of our barracks, I use Grandfather's rake to smooth the dirt. The rake is not much larger than my hand. On the island, Grandfather used it to make designs in the sand.

It is wide and flat here. We can see mountains far away, and pine trees, too. It is like the beach—no plants. But also not like the beach—no waves. So I make my own waves in the dirt with Grandfather's rake. He comes to the doorway and watches me.

"Pretty," he says.

The wind is strong, so I cannot hear well. But suddenly I think I hear Yujiin's yap in the distance. Perhaps Yujiin escaped from his crate and followed the train and chased it until it was out of sight. Perhaps he knew to stay close to the train tracks. Perhaps, after so many days, he is near us. Near enough that I can hear his yap on the wind.

I look and look and look.

But I do not see Yujiin.

And now I do not hear him either.

Grandfather motions for me to come back inside.

On our first morning in the new room, Mother rises early. Before the sun is up, she organizes it. There is a shelf on one wall where Mother stacks dishes and a tea tin and towels. Under the shelf she puts Father's tools and his fishing box. She arranges the cots so that they line the walls. She sets three suitcases on top of one another in the middle of the room to make a table. Then she drapes a sheet over it.

Mother puts the last suitcase in the corner that is away from the window and the door. She lays a pretty cloth over it and sets up our family altar. On top of the cloth, she puts a picture of Grandmother and a picture of Father's parents. She adds a shell from our beach.

Then she takes her seeds, goes outside, and plants a garden: one mound of onions, one mound of garlic, one mound of zucchini, one mound of tomatoes, one mound of cucumbers, one mound of cantaloupe.

When she's finished, she says, "Let's hope for rain."

But day after day, there is still no rain.

When she complains, Father says, "Rain will come. And in the winter there will be snow."

I remember the questions Mother couldn't answer when she said we must leave our island.

Where are we going?

Now I know: A prison in the desert. Or maybe a village in the desert.

For how long?

Now I know: Long enough to grow a garden. Or maybe even long enough to see winter.

Why?

I still do not have the answer to that question. But I can be patient.

Mother tears a blank sheet of paper from a notebook and sets it on the table with a pencil.

"This morning, Father mailed letters to Keiko and Ron," she says. "I thought maybe you would like to write them, too."

I sit at the table and look at the paper.

There are many things I would like to write:

They have taken us from the island.

They have taken Yujiin.

Grandfather does not leave our room.

I want to go home.

In the end, I write none of this. I carefully tear my paper into two pieces and write one letter to Ron and one letter to Keiko. The same message for both: *Please come.*

I stuff the letters inside the envelopes Mother gives me.

"You can post your letters at the administration building," Mother tells me. "Give them to the postman."

As I leave our room, Mother hands me two bowls to fill with water at the pump near the mess hall. She tells me it will be my job to water her garden in the morning. But first, I can mail my letters.

I put the letters in my dress pocket, leave the bowls at the pump, and walk toward the administration buildings.

The wind is strong enough to blow my hair straight up.

I hear yapping on the wind again. It sounds like Yujiin. I'm sure it is Yujiin. But I don't see him.

A man with curly dark hair is sitting behind a desk where the post office is set up. A policeman is there, too. This policeman has a face like mine. A Japanese face.

"What do you want, girl?" he asks.

I hear him, but dirt has coated my throat.

"Girl! What do you want?" he asks again. "Girl!"

I run from the building. I run down the prison-village road. I run toward the water pump where I left Mother's bowls. And now I know why I can't hear Yujiin yapping anymore. There are shadows near the water pump, shadows on the wall. And in those shadows I see Yujiin drinking from one of Mother's bowls. I run faster. But when I reach the bowl, I realize that Yujiin isn't there. Only the bowls are there. I drop to the ground to catch my breath. I don't understand. I heard Yujiin. I saw Yujiin. Where is he?

I fill the water bowls and empty them on Mother's garden. And then I remember my letters. Maybe Mother will mail them for me. I set the bowls down and reach into my pocket. But the letters are gone.

I have lost them.

MAY

Mother's seeds have sprouted. The cucumbers and zucchini were first, but the rest followed quickly. Mother added herb seeds, too. So now I watch over nine little garden mounds. One good thing about no rain: no weeds either.

It takes a lot of work to keep Mother's plants alive. By lunchtime, the sun is already so hot that I have to bring them more water so they don't shrivel up and die.

Mother checks her garden every morning and every night. The rest of the time, she talks to our neighbors and helps Mrs. Soto with her many children.

Father works from morning until night. All day long while Father's work crew builds barracks, a garbage pile grows. It holds leftover scraps—the things that are too bent or too broken or too small for them to use. At the end of the day, the work-crew fathers look over the pile and take things they might like. When they are finished the pile is almost gone.

Father gives the wood and wire and bent nails he finds to Grandfather.

Grandfather spends his days sitting by the open door on one of the chairs he made for us from the scraps. He has a frown on his face and wood or wire in his hands, making little trees and animals. Sometimes his eyes are focused on his hands. But sometimes his eyes stare into the distance. I see him: watching, waiting. I think he is looking for Yujiin, too.

Grandfather does not eat in the mess hall with everyone else. Many of the old people do not. After every meal, either Mother or I take a plate of food to our room for him.

Since Father started working, he almost never joins us at mealtimes. By the time his work crew is finished for the day, it is so late he usually eats with them. It is also late when he comes home—Father and his friends talk until the sky is black and dotted with stars.

One night after Father comes home, Mother says to him, "They need more cooks." Grandfather is already asleep, but I am still awake and sitting with Mother.

Father does not answer.

"Manami helps with my garden, so I can take this cooking job," Mother says.

"I don't know," Father says. "Until Manami is better . . ."

My neck feels prickly when Father and Mother talk about me as if I am not here.

"I need something to do," Mother says. "Stuck in this

room, I worry. Manami is silent. Father is angry. Ron and Keiko are far away. Maybe if I am busy . . ."

Father tugged my braid when Mother said my name.

"It will only be for lunch and dinner," Mother says. Her fingers touch Father's fingers. "Maybe I can make better food than what is served now?"

Father smiles. "I know you can make better food," he says.

I see Mother and Father holding hands.

So it is settled.

Father will work.

Mother will cook.

Grandfather will sit.

What will I do?

Water plants.

Sit with Grandfather.

Wait for Yujiin.

Kimmi knocks on our door the next day.

"I heard your mother will be working in the mess hall," she says. "My mother got a job, too. She's going to sew army nets at the factory when it opens next month."

Kimmi comes inside.

"Hello, Mr. Ishii," she says to Grandfather.

Grandfather nods.

"Sit," Kimmi says to me.

She brushes and braids my hair.

"Do you want to talk yet?" she asks.

I want to talk.

But I cannot talk.

"It's okay," Kimmi says. "Did you hear? They're going to start a school. In Block 7 in some of the barracks. My mother says I have to go. I want to go. And I want you to go, too. Okay? Promise?"

I nod.

Kimmi can chatter about a lot of things for a long time.

From the corner of my eye, I can see Grandfather watching Kimmi and me. I think he almost smiles when Kimmi's chatter becomes so fast that it is hard to understand her.

"Kimmi is a good friend," Grandfather tells me after she leaves. "She is happy here."

That is true. But Kimmi is always happy.

"Maybe one day you will be happy here, too," Grandfather says.

Every day, the prison-village gets more crowded. As soon as Father's work crew builds a block of barracks, newcomers fill them up. Bus after bus after bus.

These newcomers are not like my neighbors from the

island. They are from cities, not farms and fishing villages. They are from California, not Washington. And these newcomers don't always get along with my neighbors from the island.

There are so many people that I cannot keep track. I know my neighbors in Block 3. But I don't know these new people in Block 4 or 5 or 15.

Father is happy because there are plans to build a hospital and stores.

Mother is happy because there are plans to save an old apple orchard.

I think about what Kimmi told me. School.

Maybe school will be good.

But then, who will sit with Grandfather?

At least our door faces a road. When it is open, Grandfather can see and hear people and trucks going one way and then another.

But I think Grandfather is like me.

He isn't paying attention to the trucks and people.

He is looking for Yujiin.

He is waiting for Yujiin.

It is late at night, and I am supposed to be sleeping.

But I am not tired.

I open my eyes when someone knocks on our door. Mother says it is impolite to eavesdrop. She says I should shut my ears to the conversations of others.

But it is impossible when we are all living together in one room. And on this night, I am glad I do not always do what Mother says.

The voice I hear is a whisper voice, a familiar voice. It is Ron's voice.

Ron calling to us to open the door.

Father answers, his voice rumbling low.

Mother cries, the sound soft and tinkling.

Grandfather stands and walks toward the door.

I jump from bed and fling myself into my brother's arms.

I wonder if we will leave for the island tonight, or if we will wait until morning.

I wonder if we will take the train and then the boat, or if we will drive in a car that Ron has brought with him.

Before I can stretch my throat to speak, Father pulls me from Ron.

"Why did you come?" he demands.

"I had to come, Father," Ron says.

"What about school?" Father demands.

"I could not stay there knowing you are here," Ron says.

"This place is a prison!" Father says. "As long as you stayed in school you were free!"

I begin to understand. Ron has not come to save us. He has not come to take us to the island. He has not come to help me find Yujiin.

"I am glad you have come," Mother says. "It is better for us to be together."

"Keiko couldn't," Ron says. "She—"

"It is okay," Mother interrupts. "Keiko is not strong enough for this place."

"No," Ron says. "Keiko wanted to come, but we thought it is better if one of us is outside. Just in case."

My throat squeezes shut again, coated by red dirt turned to mud.

My letters, one for Ron and one for Keiko. I thought they were lost. But there was a strong wind that day. Maybe that strong wind blew my letters into the sky, all the way to Indiana.

I remember my message: *Please come.*

Not: Please come and take me from this place.

Not: Please come and take me from this place to find Yujiin.

Not: Please come and take me from this place to find Yujiin and then return to the island.

I begin to understand even more.

It is my fault that Yujiin is alone on the mainland, far from the island.

It is my fault that Grandfather has stopped laughing.

Maybe it is even my fault that Ron is with us in this prison-village, far from college.

JUNE

*R*on and Mother and I eat breakfast together at the mess hall.

"School," Mother reminds me.

Ron looks happy. He has work, too. He will teach the older children.

"I must hurry," Ron tells me, "so I won't be able to walk you to school today. Okay?"

Ron does not look at me while he waits for my response, but Mother does.

I nod and Mother says, "Okay," at the same time.

"School is a good place to talk," Ron says.

I look at my plate.

"Give her time," Mother says softly.

Does she think I cannot hear her?

Ron pats my arm. "Talk when you're ready," he says. "But school is a good place . . ."

After breakfast, Mother tells me to change into my best dress before we go to school.

There are many students and parents at Block 7. Most,

but not all, students have Japanese faces like mine. Signs with grade levels are posted on the buildings. Adults stand near the signs. Adults who are not soldiers or policemen but teachers. Many of these adults also have Japanese faces like mine. There is one adult who watches with unfriendly eyes.

"He is the warden," Mother whispers to me. "He is in charge of everyone."

Mother finds the sign that says *Grades 4, 5, and 6*, and we get in line. I am happy to see that Ron's classroom is in this barracks, too. He is standing near a sign that says *Grades 7, 8, and 9*. Three other teachers stand near this barracks, and lines have formed in front of each teacher. The high school students are in another barracks, and so are the younger children.

Finally, I am at the front of my line, and Mother presents me to the teacher. This teacher has a kind face. Her blond hair is twisted around her head. She reaches her hand toward me and smiles. I touch her hand for a second.

I know that I should tell her my name.

"Manami," Mother says for me.

Then Mother leans close to me. There is a frown on her forehead. Her eyes are sad. "All will be well," she tells me. Then she leaves.

I go inside with the teacher and the other students. This schoolroom looks like my family's room in Barracks 8. Just the furniture is different. But in this schoolroom there are no desks. Only long benches and one table with a chair.

The teacher tells us to sit down, and I am glad that Kimmi has saved the spot next to her for me.

"Just like the island," Kimmi says.

I look out the window. If it is just like the island, I would smell salt and fish. I would feel a breeze. Yujiin and Grandfather would have walked me to school. Mrs. Brown would be standing in the front of the room.

It is not just like the island.

The teacher writes her name on a large piece of white butcher paper tacked to the wall.

Miss Rosalie.

I hear my classmates repeat her name. It is beautiful. It reminds me of ocean waves rolling up and down.

Miss Rosalie passes a book around and asks us to read it to her. When Kimmi hands me the book, she whispers, "Read, Manami."

I like the words, about seeds and trees.

"Can you read this?" Miss Rosalie asks me.

Of course I can read it. I just read it.

"Manami?" Miss Rosalie asks again.

"Manami does not speak," Kimmi says.

"She cannot speak?" Miss Rosalie asks.

"Not since we came here," Kimmi says.

Miss Rosalie hands me a slate and a piece of chalk. "Can you write?"

I take the chalk and slate. I draw her name, curling like waves. I draw two eyes and a sharp nose and pointed ears.

"Yujiin," Kimmi says.

Miss Rosalie passes the book to the next student, and I set my chalk and slate on the bench beside me.

Later, when the other students go outside for recess, Miss Rosalie keeps me inside.

"I would like to be your friend, Manami," she tells me. "I wonder what you are thinking."

She points toward the administration buildings. "I live out that way," she says.

I know the doctor also lives there with his family. And other workers from the outside, too. But the soldiers who are stationed along the barbed-wire fence and in the guard towers live outside the camp.

The workers' block is like our block, with fathers and mothers and children and gardens.

But it is also different from our block.

The children in that block do not have to stay inside a wire fence. They can leave to go shopping or see a movie.

Some of those children go to our school, but the older high school students do not.

They get on a bus to go to a different school. If they wanted to, they could also follow the road to the ocean and get on a ferry and follow the ocean to the island.

For the rest of the morning, I think about this. About the other children who can go outside the fence. The other children who do not have their dogs taken away from them.

When school is dismissed at lunchtime, my classmates laugh and chatter and say goodbye to the teacher.

The boys are in a rush to leave, and they jostle me on the way out. Kimmi gives me a hug goodbye.

Just like on the island.

At the door, Miss Rosalie holds out some paper and a pencil to me.

I look down because I feel too shy to take her gift.

Her hand opens mine and places the paper and pencil in it.

That night, I take a piece of paper and prop it on my cot. It leans against the wall.

I consider drawing Miss Rosalie's name again.

Or drawing ocean waves again.

Or Yujiin's face.

Before I sleep, I put the paper and pencil under the mattress of my cot.

Perhaps I will draw tomorrow.

This is how school goes each day:

Students sit quietly.

Miss Rosalie passes a book around.

Students read from the book.

The book slides past me into the next pair of waiting hands.

Miss Rosalie writes new words on a big piece of paper, and we practice spelling them, taking turns to write the new words over and over on the slates we share. Miss Rosalie says she will bring more when she can.

We have recess, and then we work on numbers. Miss Rosalie separates us into small groups, one group in each corner of the classroom. We sit on the floor and she gives us math problems to solve on our slates. Adding, subtracting, multiplying, dividing. She makes her way from group to group.

Each day, more and more students come to classes. Ryo counts the students for Miss Rosalie.

The first day, there were twenty-one students.

After a week, the number is thirty-five.

This room is crowded with bodies on benches.

All of the rooms are crowded with bodies on benches.

It is hard for so many bodies to keep still. But we do.

For a few hours between breakfast and lunch, Miss Rosalie teaches.

When we hear the clang that announces lunch, classes are over.

Miss Rosalie stands near the doorway as students hurry to lunch lines. I stay at the back, always the last to leave.

Each day, at the door, she gives me paper.

Then I peek inside Ron's room, which is next door to Miss Rosalie's, until he waves and tells me that he will see me at dinner.

I have started to draw on Miss Rosalie's papers at home when I sit with Grandfather, and when each drawing is done I put it under my mattress with the blank paper.

I decide to give Miss Rosalie a gift.

I rise earlier than usual. Ron and Father are not home. They must have gone to the showers. Grandfather rises earlier than anyone else. I can tell by his wet hair that he has already been to the showers this morning.

Mother watches as I look through my pictures to find one for Miss Rosalie.

When I find the one I like, I write Miss Rosalie's name on it.

"For your teacher?" Mother asks. "That is a good choice."

I want to give it to her this morning before breakfast. Before the other children arrive.

With my picture in my hand, I run to Block 7 and climb the stairs to the barracks where Miss Rosalie's classroom is. I don't hear or see anyone.

Maybe Miss Rosalie is not there yet.

I wonder if I should knock on the door.

Before I decide, the door opens.

"Good morning," Miss Rosalie says.

I give her the folded paper.

Miss Rosalie unfolds it. Father's fishing boat, close to shore.

"I wondered what you might draw," she says.

It is still early enough to be very quiet. There is little wind to blow dust.

"Is this where you lived?" she asks. "It's beautiful."

On the walk back to Mother, I think about which picture I will give Miss Rosalie next.

• • •

"Manami," Mother calls one morning. "Come outside. Rain is coming."

It is still mostly dark. The mostly dark times of the day are when Mother works in her garden.

When I reach her, I squat on the ground, careful of the scraggly shoots that have begun to thicken into stems.

Mother is right. There is a new smell in the air. It is fresh and clingy and wet. Not the salty wet of the island air. Not the rusty wet of the water pump. This wet is green and sharp. This wet clears the dust from my eyes and nose. This wet is the wet of rain.

Mother is not the only one who tends a garden. Scattered around Block 3, I see others squatting among rows and mounds of struggling herbs and vegetables. It is dim, but I can see chins jutting out, lifting faces to the sky.

We all wait for the rain to come.

The sky lightens. And still we squat. Still we wait.

A loud clang breaks the stillness, calling us to the mess hall.

Ron stands in the doorway of our building.

"Breakfast," he says.

I look at Mother. Her face is still turned toward the sky.

I pick up a bowl to fill with water at the pump before we go to eat.

"Not today," she says. "Rain is coming."

Ron and I wait with Mother for a few minutes, but then we go to the mess hall alone. Father has gone ahead, and Grandfather stays in our room.

After breakfast, Ron is silent on our way to school. In his silence there is a big space that I fill up with more wet smells. I remember the itchy wet smell of sand sticking to my skin. I remember the sticky wet smell of fog. I remember the furry wet smell of Yujiin. I breathe this smell into my body. I almost feel our noses pressed together, my arms wrapped around him, his tongue licking my cheek.

"I am happy when I see you smile," Ron says.

With his words, I cannot feel Yujiin in my arms anymore.

"I will be even happier when I hear your voice," Ron says.

I look at the ground and nod. I do not want Ron to see that my smile is gone now, just like my voice.

"See you after class," he says when we get to school.

Ron does not force my chin up to see my eyes, like Mother does.

Ron does not bend down to see my eyes, like Miss Rosalie does.

Ron does not pick me up to see my eyes, like Father does.

Ron does not wait and stare at me until my eyes look up, like Grandfather does.

Ron pats my shoulder when I nod. It is enough for him.

Before classes begin, all of the students and teachers line up in front of a flagpole in the school yard. It is new. But we knew it was coming. We have been practicing for it.

Mr. Warden raises the flag.

"Salute," he booms.

I place my hand on my chest. Just like on the island. Just like Miss Rosalie had us practice.

"Pledge," he booms.

Voices drone around me.

"Girl!" Mr. Warden booms. "Pledge!"

Mr. Warden's long finger points at me.

My heart races.

Kimmi pinches my arm. "Pledge, Manami!" she says.

Mr. Warden takes heavy steps toward me.

I have a hard time catching my breath.

"Manami," Ron says.

Have they forgotten about the dust coating my throat?

"She cannot, sir," Miss Rosalie says. "She cannot speak."

Mr. Warden stares at me for a moment before stomping back to the flagpole.

When the pledge begins again, I feel Miss Rosalie's arms around my shoulders. She pulls me to her. I close my eyes.

Mr. Warden plays a song over the loudspeaker.

I listen to words about liberty and freedom, and my heartbeat slows down.

On the island, I thought I understood these words and this song. But now I am not sure.

When the song is finished and Mr. Warden has left, everyone goes into their classrooms.

"Inside, children," Miss Rosalie says. She pulls me along with her.

She stands in front of the class while we find our seats.

"As I read, think about changes in nature as spring turns into summer," she says. "You may use a slate to draw, if you'd like."

When the slate basket passes down my row, I take a slate and a piece of chalk.

It is not normal for our classroom to be so silent.

A slate bangs to the floor and many children jump.

If Mother were here, she would say, "All will be well."

Miss Rosalie does not say, "All will be well."

She reads poems about spring and summer and honey-bees and budding flowers. My hand flits over my slate, dipping and bobbing, scratching and resting. Chalk feathers from one line to another, circling and looping until I am finished.

"Beautiful," Miss Rosalie says when she picks up my slate. She bends down to look into my eyes. "This is how I picture the seasons changing, too."

The school day ends, and the rain has not come. But I can still smell the promise of it.

On the island, rain is not an all-day promise in the air. Rain comes, rain goes. Sometimes rain pounds hard and heavy. Sometimes rain mists soft and gentle. But it doesn't hover and wait, holding itself just out of reach.

Before I leave school, I go to Ron's classroom. I have more paper from Miss Rosalie in my hand.

He is speaking to three wild boys who are his students. They are older than me and they scare me. I cannot hear Ron's words, but I can see his frown. When he sees me in the doorway, he motions me forward.

"Come in, Manami," he says. His frown changes to a smile.

The wild boys leave.

"May I see your picture?" Ron asks.

I hand him a blank piece of paper.

"Hmm," he says. He turns the paper one way and then

another. "Perhaps," he says. He turns the paper to the other side. "Oh, yes," he says. "I see it now."

I hear a quiet laugh from behind me, and I turn to look.

Miss Rosalie stands in the doorway.

"I'm sorry to interrupt," she says, turning to go.

"Please come in," Ron says.

Ron hands the paper to me. Then he stands behind me and puts his hands on both of my shoulders.

"Thank you, Miss Rosalie," he says. "Thank you for speaking up for Manami this morning."

Miss Rosalie's face turns red.

"You're welcome," she says.

Ron turns me around. "I must prepare lessons for to-morrow."

On my walk from school to home, I see the wild boys huddled against the wall of a building in Block 9. Kimmi waves to me from a group of girls lined up in front of the mess hall in our block.

Before I eat lunch, I check on Grandfather.

He sits in a chair near the door.

I sit on the ground next to him and take his hand in mine. Grandfather's hands are large and thin. They are hard and soft all at once. I squeeze his hand, and he squeezes back. I press his hand against my cheek, then squeeze it one more time before I go to the mess hall. Mother will worry if I am late. I am not hungry, but I fill my plate with food. I will take it to Grandfather.

When Mother comes out of the kitchen and sees that I am alone, she says, "Go sit with the other children. When you are done, you can take something to Grandfather."

I do as she says and sit with the other children, but as soon as she goes inside the kitchen, I pick up my plate and hurry back to Grandfather.

After he finishes eating, I draw pictures on Miss Rosalie's paper for him. Once, I drew Yujiin. But Grandfather would not look. Now I draw the ocean. Waves, sand, shells. Grandfather looks. But he does not smile.

I draw footprints in wet sand. Grandfather's large, firm footprints, followed by my smaller bare feet.

But my picture is not right. Not yet. I smear some sand here, smear other sand there. Yujiin is there, too.

I hold the picture up to Grandfather's face. His eyes are closed.

I take out a new sheet of paper and draw Mother's garden. I am so busy with my pictures that I don't realize it is time for dinner until Ron comes inside. I look up when he calls my name.

While I stack my papers and pencil, I hear the clanging call from the mess hall.

The mess hall line is not long. After we fill our plates, Mother motions for us to sit at a table where there is just enough space for us at the end of a bench. Ron and I are careful to arrive early for dinner so that we can eat with Mother. She has a short break to eat with us.

Mother goes to the kitchen and brings three cups and a steaming teapot.

She is saving the last of our tea, so we drink hot water every evening with our dinner. Some people still have tea to drink, but most do not. Many do not drink hot water either. But Mother brings her teapot out every night.

Before we have time to take even one bite or one sip, a flash lights up the sky, followed by a crash.

"Finally, the rain!" Mother says.

She grabs my hand and drags me to the door. Ron follows. Others crowd behind us.

And then the rain comes.

Mother pulls us outside. She holds my hands, spinning us around and around. Others join in our rain dance. The yard in front of the mess hall is a muddy swirl of people.

The rain does not drip or drop. The rain pours. Like the water pump. Like the showers.

It pours until the laughing faces and twirling feet stop their happy dance.

It pours until Mother begins to frown.

"Hurry, children!" she says. "We must save my plants."

We run to Mother's garden. The water pours so fast that there is already a pond forming in the yard.

Mother touches her battered plants one by one.

The pouring rain has pounded them into the ground. Fragile stems are broken. Tiny leaves float free.

Mother kneels and pulls me to her, wrapping her arms around my waist. She cries into my stomach.

And still the rain pours.

Ron joins Mother on the ground.

And then, as quick as it started, the rain stops.

"We will save them," Ron promises Mother.

"They cannot be saved," Mother says.

"We will try," Ron promises again.

He helps Mother stand and leads her back to the mess hall.

"What is this place?" I hear her say.

I stay behind, touching the cilantro plant at my feet. Its stem is thinner than my little finger and longer than my forearm. But it lies flat against the ground. I lift it, but it falls. I prop it with two stones, but it is not enough. I dig into the mud with my fingers, searching for more stones. I have barely scraped the top layer of mud away when I see that the dirt underneath is not wet. It is hard and dry. All that pouring and still I will have to bring water from the pump for the thirsty plants.

I pry two more stones from the hard dirt.

I fill a bowl of water at the pump and pour it at the base of the plant.

Now I wonder: What is this place?

I look around Mother's garden. There are more plants to save.

I make a promise: This garden will not die.

Ron finds me in the garden, my hands thick with mud.

"There you are," he says. "Come on. You need to eat dinner. Then I'll help you with this."

Later that week, we are all surprised when Father joins us for dinner.

Mother and Ron and I are sitting down when Father enters the mess hall. Ron apologizes for our having already started to eat. I scoot down the bench to make room. Mother pours steaming water into her cup and sets it in front of Father.

Father does not have a plate.

"Would you like me to get you some food?" Mother asks.

"I'll eat in a minute," he says. Father rests his hand on his chest. Then he pulls an envelope from the inside of his shirt.

"A letter from Keiko," he says, handing it to Mother.

Mother reads quickly. "No," she says, and passes it to Ron.

Ron reads slowly.

"Father," he says. "I cannot."

"This will prove that you are American," Father says.

"Why must I prove it?" Ron asks. "I know what is in my head and in my heart."

Father and Ron stare at each other.

Many others at our table stare, too. When they see that I notice their stares, they look away.

Father leaves the mess hall.

He does not eat rice and chicken with us. He does not drink his hot water.

"Mother," Ron says.

"I understand," she says. "I do not wish it either."

I am curious, but I can be patient.

After we eat, Mother returns to the kitchen to finish her work shift.

"Keiko suggests I join the army," Ron whispers. "There are rumors that soon the army will welcome those of us who are living here. Keiko says that if I join the army, I will be free to leave this place. But what kind of freedom is that? Should I fight for the army that imprisons my family?"

It is like old times. Ron tells me what Mother and Father do not want me to hear.

Ron hands me a slip of paper.

"This is for you," he says.

"Dear Sister," it reads. "I know you are a comfort to Mother. Study and learn so that one day you can live with me and go to college. Keiko."

Once, I wanted to live with Keiko and go to college.

Now I just want to go back to the island.

JULY

For many days, Miss Rosalie and the other teachers have been preparing us for the Independence Day celebration. Some students learn poems. Some students learn songs. I make a banner. The older students will recite part of the Declaration of Independence.

On Independence Day, everyone gathers in the open space on the other side of the classrooms in Block 7. Ron says there are plans to build an auditorium in that open space.

Mr. Warden is there.

My island neighbors from Block 3 are there.

People from all of the blocks are there: students, parents, grandparents.

I think I have never seen so many people in one place before.

Miss Rosalie told us that there are now almost ten thousand people living in this prison-village.

Ten thousand people with hair and skin like mine.

Ten thousand people with Japanese names like mine.

Students line up in front, facing the parents and grandparents.

I stand next to Kimmi.

Mr. Warden motions to one of the teachers to begin.

The teacher nods and a high school student steps forward. "Salute!" he shouts above the crowd.

All of the students salute.

But I feel nervous when I see that some adults in the crowd do not salute.

"Pledge!" the high school boy shouts.

Students recite the Pledge of Allegiance.

But I feel nervous when I see that many adults in the crowd do not pledge.

Maybe they do not know the Pledge of Allegiance.

Or maybe they do.

Mr. Warden must not see them, though, because he doesn't leave his spot. After the pledge, he reads a speech from a paper. But the wind starts to blow and dust fills my ears, so I cannot hear his words.

After the ceremony, school is dismissed for lunch and the crowd shrinks. We go back to our own blocks. Back to our own barracks. Ron walks me to lunch, the wind pushing our arms and legs toward the mess hall.

On the other side of the road that separates Block 3 from Block 9, some men huddle in the shadows of one of the barracks. These men are city men, not from our island.

Ron sees me staring.

"Come," he says. But then he stops and looks.

I see what he sees: some of the wild boys from his class are lurking on the edges of the men in the shadows.

"Go to lunch, Manami," Ron says.

My stomach tightens. I do not want to leave Ron alone with these men and the wild boys.

Ron gently pushes my back. "I'll be there in a minute," he says.

I walk as slowly as I can, looking over my shoulder at the shadow group.

As Ron nears them, I see a man give a paper to one of the wild boys. The paper gets crumpled and shoved into his pocket.

I am too far to hear Ron's conversation with the wild boys, but I hear some words: Lunchtime. Go to the mess hall.

I am relieved when I see Ron walk away from that group, a few of the wild boys slinking behind him.

• • •

The wind has not stopped blowing for more than a week.

It is heavy and hot and dry. Island winds can be heavy, too, but they are cool and wet. Island winds coat my face with tiny beads of water. This wind pelts my face with dust. It glues my eyelashes closed until Mother presses a warm, wet cloth on my eyes to clean the dust away. It powders my hair until Mother brushes the dust free with her long, strong strokes. It layers my tongue and throat. Too much for Mother to clean out. Not even two cups of hot water from the teapot can clean it out.

But just below the howl of the wind, I can hear another sound. It is not quite a whimper and not quite a growl. It is something in between. Yujiin is out there in the dusty wind. I hear him when I walk to the water pump in the morning. I hear him when I sit in the garden. I hear him when I wait at the mess hall for Mother.

I am afraid for Yujiin.

What if no one let him out of that crate?

What if he is roaming the streets looking for me?

What if he found a ferryboat to the island and is waiting at our house because Pastor Rob does not know he has returned?

And the worst: What if he followed the train tracks and is lost in the dusty wind?

When Miss Rosalie hands me paper at the end of the school day, I get an idea.

If the wind was strong enough to carry my letter to Ron, then maybe it is strong enough to bring Yujiin.

When I get home, I draw Yujiin on a piece of paper. I do not know what he looks like now, so I draw him as I last saw him, shoved into a crate. I draw his eyes and his ears and his tail. His mouth open and barking. His paws pushing against the crate.

I fill the drawing with promise words:

Come, Yujiin, and I will give you an extra bowl of rice and chicken.

Come, Yujiin, and we will run until we fall down.

Come, Yujiin, and you can sleep in my bed.

In the morning, I rise early. I water Mother's garden and check each of the plants. Since the rainstorm they have grown tall again. Then I walk past Block 3, toward the administration buildings. I walk behind the buildings until there is nothing but dirt and sky between me and the fence that surrounds the prison-village. I hold up my picture of Yujiin and make a wish, raising my arm high above my head. The wind flaps the paper. Then it rips it from my hand, carrying it over the fence. I watch my paper until it is too far away to see.

I have added my paper promises to the air.

After school, I draw another picture of Yujiin. This time, I draw him as he looked hidden beneath my coat. His panting tongue. His wide-open eyes. Crouched and quiet.

I write more promise words on this drawing:

Come, Yujiin. Come. We will take long walks and wrap up in a blanket together.

The next morning, when I release this drawing in the wind, it flies higher than yesterday's paper.

Every day, I draw Yujiin. Some days it is one picture. Some days it is more.

Yujiin running on the sand.

Yujiin sleeping under Grandfather's chair.

Yujiin watching seabirds dip and bob.

Yujiin waiting by the door.

Each morning, I make a wish for Yujiin to come and I send new promises in the air.

After ten and then twenty and then thirty drawings, I wonder. One of my pictures should have found Yujiin by now. So why hasn't he come?

I draw one last picture. Yujiin and Grandfather. Sitting side by side on their rock at the beach. The ocean in front of them. The sun behind them. This will be the one, I think. This will be the one that brings Yujiin.

When I release this picture the next morning, I do not write a promise. I write a message instead: *I'm sorry, Yujiin! I'm sorry.*

I hold it up high. Then I jump and throw it into the wind.

Wind and dust and tears fill my eyes. I scrub at them with my sleeve and run home. Past people on their way to work. Past Mother's garden.

Inside our room, I drop to the floor at Grandfather's feet. I wrap my arms around his legs and try to speak. But my throat is still closed. I want to tell him I am sorry. I want to ask him to forgive me. But no words come out.

"I know you miss Yujiin," Grandfather says. "I miss him, too."

I cry until I feel Grandfather's hand on my head. I look up and he moves his hand to my cheek. I scrub at my eyes again.

"I know you are sorry," Grandfather says. "I am sorry, too."

Ron has already left for school, and classes have started. But my heart feels like flying when Grandfather takes my hand and walks me to school.

That night, Grandfather and Ron and I sit at a long table in the mess hall. Grandfather leans his head toward Ron, who is speaking to him. There is no mention of secrets in Ron's words, so I stop listening. Instead, I keep my eyes fixed on the entrance to the kitchen. This is the first time Grandfather has come to the mess hall. Mother does not know about Grandfather's decision, and I want to see her when she learns.

Mother comes out, balancing a teapot and cups. She takes several steps before she sees. Then she stops walking.

I touch Grandfather's arm.

Ron stops talking.

Mother starts walking.

She sets the teapot and cups on the table.

I can see tears on her cheeks.

I also see her smile.

It is a small smile. A quiet smile. But it is the first smile I have seen on Mother's face since we left the island.

"Father," Mother says. "You're here."

Grandfather nods. "I am here."

I lift the teapot to pour hot water into the cups, but Mother stops my hand.

"Wait," she says. She leaves the table, walking so quickly she is almost running. She leaves the mess hall. In a few minutes, she returns, carrying a bowl and a cup as well as a small sack in her arms.

Mother sits at the table and places the teapot in front of

her and one cup next to it. She sets the bowl to her left. She bows over the table.

I remember this from the island. It is a special ceremony. A ceremony to honor a special moment. Mother is preparing tea.

Grandfather sits up straight.

Ron and I place our hands on our laps.

Many pieces of the ceremony are missing.

There is no special mat to cover the table. Instead, Mother folds her napkin and sets it on the table.

There is no special tea set. But Mother pours water into the cup in front of her, swirling it around to clean it before pouring it into the empty bowl. She dries the cup with a napkin.

There is no special tea powder to whisk into boiling water. Instead, Mother shakes the last of the tea leaves from the sack into the teapot. She pours the weak tea from the teapot into the cup. She holds the cup on her palm and then places it on the table in front of Grandfather. Grandfather holds the cup in his palm and sips. He sips again before placing the cup on the table. Then he takes a napkin and wipes the rim of the cup.

Ron takes the cup in his palm and sips. After he has set the cup on the table and wiped the rim, it is my turn.

I am careful to do as Mother has taught me. I place the cup on the palm of my left hand and raise my palm to my chest. I sip slowly.

This weak tea washes the dust from my throat.

Perhaps tonight I will find my voice.

Father joins us in our room earlier than usual this evening. He looks excited.

I remember the last time Father looked excited. It was when he pulled Keiko's letter from his pocket.

That was many Yujiin pictures ago. I think about this morning's picture—the picture with a message. I wonder how long it will take for that picture to find Yujiin.

This time Father does not pull a letter from inside his shirt.

This time he pulls something furry and small and brown from inside his shirt.

He places it on the floor of our room.

"This dog needs a home," Father says. "I saw him by an administration building. He's little, like Yujiin. I thought maybe it would help. Maybe bring back Manami's voice. I asked a soldier if we could have the dog. The soldier said the dog didn't belong to anyone. It just wandered in through the gate. He said I could have it."

My heart starts to beat so hard that I think it might beat out of my chest.

Ron pets the dog.

Mother brings a bowl of water.

"Hello," Grandfather says. He smiles when a pink tongue licks his hand.

I hear Father's laugh and see Grandfather's smile.

Mother looks up at me and her smile freezes. She reaches toward me.

"Manami?" she asks. "Do you want a dog?"

I do want a dog. I want my dog. I want Yujiin.

The wind gave my message to the wrong dog. If this dog got Yujiin's message, then how will Yujiin find me?

I want to explain, but my throat closes tight. Too tight for words to get out. Too tight for air to get in. I run outside to Mother's garden.

I sit on the ground between mounds of zucchini and cilantro.

I touch the thickening stems.

I touch the handprint-shaped leaves.

My throat begins to open just a little bit. Just enough for air to get in.

I close my eyes when I see Father walk out the door carrying the dog.

The next morning, I see the dog following behind Kimmi's mother.

At school, Kimmi tells me how happy she is that my father gave them the dog.

I want to be happy for Kimmi, but I cannot smile. After a minute, I nod.

AUGUST

The wind that blows sand so hard that it hurts my cheeks finally stops. But the sun grows hot and heavy and burns everything in the prison-village: faces, necks, hands, plants.

For several weeks, there will be no classes. Workers will use the time to make new classrooms. The high school classes will continue to be in Block 7, but the elementary and junior high school classes will be spread out in many blocks. When school starts again, we will all still meet in the school yard in front of Block 7 for the pledge.

There are also some other new buildings in the prison-village. It is starting to look like a town. Except for the wire fence.

Workers have just finished building a hospital.

A store opened. Mother can buy fabric and shoes. The store sells everything—besides fabric and shoes, you can buy furniture and dishes and toys and tools.

Ron asks me to meet him at school. Miss Rosalie is leaving for the school vacation, and she would like to say goodbye to me.

I would also like to say goodbye to Miss Rosalie. And I wish to give her a gift. I pull my drawings out from under my mattress and look through them. There are three pictures I like.

The first is a drawing of the school during recess.

The second is a drawing of Miss Rosalie reading a poem to the class.

The third is a drawing of me and Ron and Grandfather in Mother's garden.

Because I cannot choose, I take them all.

When I arrive, I see Miss Rosalie sitting on the steps outside the classroom. Ron stands in the doorway behind her, frowning.

I wonder what has made Ron unhappy.

"Here's Manami," Ron says.

I hand Miss Rosalie the three drawings. She looks at them all quickly and then looks at the picture of her reading a poem for a long time.

"This is very good," she says. "But I think you know that."

Miss Rosalie studies the drawing.

"Do I really do that with my hair?" she asks.

I nod. Yes, I think. You do. You do twirl your hair with your finger when you read poetry to us.

Then she pulls out the drawing of Mother's garden.

"I shall treasure this most of all," she says. "I will look at it every day and think of Manami. Manami who loves her family. Manami who grows a garden. Manami who draws beautifully."

I look down because I do not want Miss Rosalie to see my sorrow. I will miss her.

Miss Rosalie leans down until she can see my eyes.

"I'm just visiting my aunt and uncle for a few weeks," she says. "I will come back."

Miss Rosalie says it like a promise.

I nod.

"I have a gift for you, too," Miss Rosalie says.

She goes inside her classroom and returns with a thick stack of paper and four pencils.

I lift my eyes to Miss Rosalie's face and am surprised to see tears on her cheeks. For the second time, Miss Rosalie wraps her arms around my shoulders.

"I will miss you," she whispers. "But I will come back."

Ron tells me to walk home without him.

On my way, I see Kimmi's dog lying in the shade in front of their barracks.

As I walk past the mess hall, I see another dog following a man. This dog is white. But it is large. When I see this new dog, my heart starts to beat faster. Why did this dog also come and not Yujiin? I run the rest of the way home.

When I burst through the door, Grandfather jumps from his chair and I drop my paper and pencils.

"What is wrong?" he asks.

My breath comes quickly after that run. I cover my eyes with my hands.

Grandfather lifts me and sets me in his chair. "Breathe," he says.

When my breath is calm again, Grandfather says, "Tell me what has happened."

I open my mouth, but words do not come out. My eyes burn with tears, and I close them.

Grandfather places a pencil in my hand and sets a piece of paper on my lap.

"I must know what has upset you, little one," Grandfather says. "Is it because your teacher is leaving?"

I shake my head no.

I think about the Yujiin drawings. I think about the promises I made. I wonder if these two dogs found my Yujiin drawings by mistake. And came to the prison-village because of them.

I open my eyes, but Grandfather is blurry. The room is blurry. When I write, even my letters are blurry: *Dogs.*

"I understand," Grandfather says. "They make you miss Yujiin more."

He takes the paper and pencil from me and then sends me to my bed.

"No drawing," he says. "Sleep."

When I wake, it is nearly dark. I have slept for hours and missed dinner. Grandfather and Mother and Father and Ron gather around the small table, speaking in low voices. I sit up on my bed.

Mother joins me, unbraiding my hair and brushing it out. The rhythm of the brushing almost makes me fall asleep again. She brings a wet cloth to clean my face and hands. It feels cool against my skin. I hold it to my forehead while she braids my hair.

"I'm sorry the dogs upset you today," she says. "Come."

I sit between Ron and Grandfather.

Ron tells Mother that I went to the school to say goodbye to Miss Rosalie.

"Miss Rosalie is fond of Manami," he says.

"Manami is a good student," Mother says. "I am not surprised."

"Yes," says Father. "Manami is a good girl. We are proud of her."

"Manami brought paper and pencils home," says Grandfather.

"They were a gift from Miss Rosalie," Ron says.

I feel my cheeks heat up. This praise makes me feel happy and uncomfortable at the same time.

Mother uncovers a bowl of rice and places it before me. She slices a cucumber and arranges it on a plate in the shape of ocean waves. She pours water from a teapot into a cup.

The water is not hot. It is also not cold. But the cup feels good in my hands. Solid. The cucumber is cool and sweet. The rice is filling.

While I eat, Ron and Father talk. Ron wants Father to find a place for him on his building crew until school starts again. Father does not want Ron to work on the building crew. Father wants Ron to spend his time studying so that he will not fall behind when he returns to college. When their talk is almost an argument, Mother interrupts.

"My garden is strong and healthy," she says.

"You brought good seeds," Father says.

"This desert sun is hard on the plants," Mother says. "They would have died if not for Manami and Ron's help."

Father again tells Ron to use this month to study. Before Ron can answer, Grandfather speaks.

"No arguments tonight," he says.

Mother fills the silence that follows with a song.

With no school, the wild boys run loose. They do not study. They do not garden. They do not work. They huddle in shadows. They scowl. They smoke cigarettes.

Grandfather says, "Their fathers are working and cannot take them out on boats."

Grandfather says, "Their mothers are working and cannot watch over them."

Grandfather says, "They are running wild."

I think, My father is working.

I think, My mother is working.

I think, I do not run wild.

Ron buys a baseball bat, a baseball, and a glove with his salary. He makes a baseball diamond. He gets wood squares from Father for each base.

It stays light past 8:00 p.m. So after dinner, Ron picks up his bat and ball and glove.

"Baseball?" Ron asks me.

I look at the ground because I do not want to disappoint Ron. But I do not want to play ball with the wild boys.

"Maybe next time," he says.

He tosses his ball in the air with one hand and catches it with the other while he walks to the baseball diamond.

From the spot in Mother's garden where I squat to

check for tomato bugs, I see one wild boy after another slink from the shadows to follow Ron.

"That is good," Grandfather says.

I disagree. I do not like to see those wild boys with Ron.

On the island, August is not hot the way it is in this prison-village. Here, there is a time during the day that is so hot that I cannot move. So hot that sweat films over my entire body. So dry that my lungs hurt to breathe. So bright that my eyes burn.

It is during this time of the day that Mother tells me to lie on my bed. If I am still, the heat is not as bad. And sometimes I can fall asleep. If I cannot be still, then I draw. And I forget about being hot.

It is during this time of the day that Grandfather tells me stories of his childhood. He wasn't born on the same island I was, but on a different one: Japan. He tells me stories about my grandmother. He tells me the story of a great wave taller than a building that destroyed an entire village when he was a boy.

It is also during this hottest month of the year that we light lanterns to honor and remember our ancestors. The celebration brings our whole family together. At home we always sent our lanterns down a creek. They floated in a sparkly line: the first one was Mother's to honor Grandmother, then Grandfather's to honor his parents, then Father's to honor his parents, and then Ron's, Keiko's, and mine. Ours honored our long-ago ancestors.

We ate sweets. We danced. We drummed.

I wore a beautiful kimono and carried a painted fan.

This year, I wonder: Where will we send our lanterns? There are no creeks to carry them away.

As it gets closer to the time to light lanterns, Mother and Father stay out late to help prepare for the celebration.

But one night, Father wakes me up and hands me a narrow package wrapped in bright, silky fabric. I think it must be pencils. I untie the knot and fold the fabric back. Father has made a fan for me.

I trace my fingers along the smooth spokes of the fan. A red cord hangs from the base of the spokes. When I open it, the paper changes from white to green to blue. Father has painted a boat and our island. The white wall of our house. My favorite rock.

It makes me happy and sad at the same time.

I kiss Father's cheek.

He pats my arm.

"Go to sleep now," Mother says.

I wrap Father's fan in the bright fabric and put it under my bed.

In the morning, I show Grandfather my fan. He inspects it as if he has never seen it before.

"You know," he says, "your father spent many hours making this for you."

I know.

"You see," he says, "your father thinks of the island just like you."

I see.

"You understand," he says, "your father loves you very much."

I understand.

"We will make lanterns," Grandfather says. "Lanterns and a drum."

Grandfather and I take a long walk to Father's work crew. There have been no newcomers for a week. This is good because there is no place to put newcomers anymore. Every barracks is filled. Since they have finished building barracks, Father and his crew have been working on building a barn and fences for cows, pens for hogs, and coops for chickens that the government is sending to us. Some of the animals have already arrived.

I see men working in the pasture. And two new dogs who are not Yujiin.

Grandfather sees them and squeezes my hand.

When we get near Father's work site, he leaves his crew to meet us.

Father and Grandfather speak in low voices while I watch the crew build the barn's roof. The cow barn has only three walls. The chicken coops have four walls. I think I like the three-wall barn better. The cows can come and go whenever they want. The chickens are stuck inside their coops until someone lets them out for the day.

Grandfather hands me a bundle of wood pieces to take back to our room. He carries his own bundle, along with two tools.

When we get home, Grandfather stacks the wood and lays the tools on the ground near the steps in front of our barracks.

"Wedge," he says.

It is wide and flat on one end and narrows to a sharp line on the other.

"Knife," he says.

It is as long as my forearm, with handles sticking straight up on both ends.

Grandfather sets a piece of wood on the ground and places the wedge on top. He taps the wedge with a hammer until the piece of wood splits into two pieces. When he has split all of the wood, Grandfather sits on a stair step. He holds a split piece of wood between his feet. With his hands around the handles of the knife, he slowly pulls the knife toward him, shaving off a strip of wood. He does this over and over until he has a stack of strips on the step next to him.

Grandfather cuts the strips into pieces about the same size as my pencils.

Grandfather dips his finger into a small pot and smears sticky glue onto some of the wood strips, joining them to make the frame of a box. Then he glues two more strips on the bottom of the box to make an *X*. He sets the frame aside and makes another.

"Bring paper," Grandfather says.

From underneath my mattress, I get half of the stack of paper that Miss Rosalie gave me.

"Go ahead and paint," Grandfather says. "With your paintings, the lanterns for our family will be the most beautiful lanterns."

I pick up the chicken-feather paintbrush Grandfather has laid over the top of a bowl of black paint.

I want the first painting for the first lantern to be for

Grandmother. I dip the paintbrush into the paint and carefully paint the roots of a tree. I am not used to painting with chicken-feather paintbrushes. But after a few strokes, my painting becomes easier.

Grandfather watches me. As soon as I paint the first upward stroke of the tree's branches, he nods and goes back to his gluing.

Grandfather knows that a plum tree is for Grandmother. Like her plum trees on the island.

When I finish, I set the paper aside so the paint can dry.

I want my next lantern paper to be for Yujiin.

Grandfather watches me again. As soon as I paint the first round, dark eye, he stands up and walks away.

But I do not stop. I do not try to comfort him. This is something I know, something I have learned: it is not possible to comfort Grandfather about Yujiin. I know this because I know that I cannot be comforted about Yujiin. So I paint. I paint and I think.

I do not understand why, if my drawings are being found by other dogs, Yujiin cannot find one.

But maybe this lantern will shine so bright that Yujiin will see it and know that I miss him. And maybe he will come. Maybe.

So I paint a lantern for Grandmother and a lantern for Yujiin.

I paint more pictures for our ancestors.

I hear a clang calling us to lunch.

But I continue to paint.

And Grandfather glues.

He glues the painted papers onto the frames.

Together, we make lanterns.

I am hungry when the last lantern is painted and glued.

Grandfather and I walk to the mess hall. Mother is inside the kitchen. She and other mothers and grandmothers have been working longer than usual for the last three days to make special treats: trays of salty-sour rice balls, stacks of crunchy cookies, bowls of honey-covered nuts.

"Your daughter is hungry," Grandfather says.

"Is my father hungry, too?" Mother asks.

"Perhaps," Grandfather says.

"I will see what I can do," Mother says. "Next time, my daughter should eat during mealtime."

"She will," Grandfather says. He winks at me. We sit at a table to wait for Mother.

Mother brings us a tray that is covered with a thin white cloth.

Grandfather carries the tray to our room. When he removes the cloth, my stomach makes a happy growl.

A steaming teapot, a bowl of rice, sliced cucumbers and melon, four of the crunchy cookies, and two salty-sour rice balls.

I lift the teapot and as I begin to pour into Grandfather's cup, I almost drop it. Instead of just hot water, Mother has given us actual tea. I pour slowly, afraid to spill even one drop.

"Ahhh," Grandfather says, lifting his cup to his mouth.

I hold my cup near my face, breathing in the leafy bark scent of the tea. I let the first sip of hot tea sit in my mouth for a second. I feel its bitter, dark taste on the back of my tongue. It is not green and sharp like the tea Mother used to keep on the island. But it is tea. And it is good. When I swallow, the tea begins to wash away the dust coating my throat. I sip again and again.

"This tea is a treat for the celebration," Grandfather says while we eat. "Many of our neighbors worked together to save money to buy it."

When we finish eating, I fill my cup again.

Grandfather raises his eyebrows.

I pick up my cup and walk to the door.

Grandfather understands.

"Wear your hat," he says, putting it on my head.

I hold the cup out in front of me, safe between my two hands. By the time I reach Father's work crew, the tea is no longer hot. Father does not see me, but another man notices me standing beneath Father's ladder and shouts to him.

He climbs down the ladder and puts his arm around my shoulders and leads me away from the work crew.

I offer the cup to Father.

He takes it and looks inside. He blinks many times before he takes a sip. When Father has finished his tea, he places the cup in my hands.

"Thank you," he says. He pulls on my braid and then returns to work.

During the long walk to Father's work crew, I did not think about the hot, bright sun. I did not think about the sweat dripping down my back. I did not think about my tired legs.

But now, walking back, I feel the hot, bright sun beating down on my head and arms. I feel new rivers of sweat dripping down my back. I am itchy where my dress sticks to my skin. And my legs are so tired that I can only lift one foot after the other by counting my steps home.

Grandfather waits for me in the slim line of shade in front of our barracks. He has a stack of wood pieces next to him. They are about the size of one of Miss Rosalie's books. Grandfather rubs the edges of one piece of wood smooth, shaping his drum.

I sit on the step next to Grandfather, take off my hat, and wipe the sweat from my forehead. After I catch my breath, I go inside to pour another cup of tea.

Grandfather puts my hat back on my head as I walk down the steps.

On this walk, all I can think about is how sweaty I am, how hot the sun is, how tired my legs are. But I hold the cup of tea in front of my body, carefully hidden inside my hands.

The walk to Block 7 is not long. Since Father wouldn't let him join his work crew, Ron found a job building things for the new classrooms. I find him making benches in the school yard.

Ron stops working as soon as he sees me. He looks at my sweaty face. He takes the cup from my hands and pulls me under a shady spot.

"Sit," he says. Then he sips his tea.

"Hot tea is just what I need right now," he says. "How did you know?"

I just knew.

"Father does not like me working," he says.

He sips.

"But the extra money will be helpful," he says.

He sips.

"I cannot sit around until school starts," he says. "I will study at night."

He sips.

"One day, we will leave this place," he says.

He hands me his empty cup.

"Thank you, Sister," he says. "You are a good listener."

Ron's smile makes my heart swell inside my chest. I run all the way home. Sitting on the step next to Grandfather, I remember that the sun is hot and my legs are tired.

Grandfather sends me inside to rest.

The first two nights of the celebration, the mess hall is crowded with our neighbors from Block 3. One table is covered with a red cloth. On top of the red cloth are bright flowers made from newspaper and folded fabrics. Lanterns are stacked on the floor, lining the walls. Vegetables are cut into pretty shapes: butterflies, flowers, and birds.

We eat the vegetables and rice balls and melons and cookies. When the sun goes down, we gather in the large open space next to Block 3. I can see around the camp that a few of the other blocks have dancing and drumming, too.

Grandfather brings the drum he made. It is a square block with rounded edges. His drum clacks when he hits it with a wooden stick. Others bring drums, too. Some are home-made like Grandfather's. Some have a metal side that sounds almost like a bell when it is hit. Some are large and round and covered with stretched leather. People dance and drum and laugh. I watch until Grandfather says it's time to go home for bed.

But the third night, the final night when we light our lanterns, starts off more seriously.

Mother comes home from work early and takes me to the women's showers.

Father and Grandfather and Ron go to the men's showers.

Mother dresses me in a kimono of green silk embroidered with pink flowers that she had packed at the bottom of her suitcase. She dresses in her own kimono. It is cream silk embroidered with pink and brown flowers.

Mother combs my hair, fastening it at the back of my neck. Then she pulls her own hair back.

Father and Grandfather and Ron do not wear silk robes. They wear their best suits even though it is so hot.

Mother motions for me to sit on the floor beside Ron. She sits on the floor between Father and Grandfather.

We face our family altar. A framed photo of Grandmother is joined by carved fruit and paper flowers. A glass jar filled halfway with sand holds a candle, the flame shining against the jar's glass.

I think of Grandmother. I never met the other ancestors, but Grandmother was quiet and strong. She made the softest salty-sour rice balls. She drew pictures for me in the sand—pictures of flowers decorated with rocks and shells, pictures of sea lions and boats, and my name. Grandmother's hands smelled like cucumbers and herbs. Her smile was small and warm.

I wonder if Grandmother's spirit knows we are in this prison-village and not on the island.

When it is time to stand up, I take a deep breath. The smell of cucumbers fills my nose.

We eat at the mess hall and then go outside to the open space for more dancing and drumming. Kimmi runs up to me and grabs my hands. "Dance with me," she says.

She spins us in a circle, and we dance until she asks, "Do you want to get some cookies?"

We go to the mess hall, with its door wide open and tables covered with food. I pick up a rice ball, and Kimmi picks up three crunchy cookies.

A grandmother brings a fresh pot of tea from the kitchen, but I am too hot from dancing and running to drink tea. Kimmi and I drink water from our cups after we finish eating, and then we go back outside.

There is a group of girls giggling and dancing, and Kimmi pulls me toward them. But I do not want to join these girls. Sometimes, these girls look at me like I am strange. I see Grandfather setting our lanterns on the steps leading to our barracks, and I run to join him.

When the sky is completely black, Mother lights a short candle. She uses it to melt wax from the bottom of another candle, letting the wax drip onto the middle of the cross that covers the bottom of the lantern for Yujiin. Mother sticks the candle into the pool of hot wax and hands it to me. Next, she prepares Ron's lantern and Father's lantern and Grandfather's lantern and, finally, her own. We take our lanterns to join the other families in the open space where candlelit lanterns are set here and there on the ground.

I raise my lantern high over my head. For many minutes, I watch Yujiin's dark eyes look down on me. Then I place the lantern on the ground with everyone else's and I think, Maybe Yujiin will see. From far away, maybe he will see the flickering lights. Maybe he will know I am thinking of him.

Then someone starts a steady drumbeat. It is deeper than the clack of the drum Grandfather made. A rush of wind makes the candlelight flicker and sputter.

My heart drops. The flame from Yujiin's lantern is gone.

SEPTEMBER

As soon as I hear that Miss Rosalie has returned, I run to the school. It takes me a while to figure out which is her new classroom. But I peek in windows until I see a familiar stack of books on a table. Miss Rosalie is not there, but I go inside the building and slide a painting of lanterns spilling across the ground under her classroom door. I think she will like this painting.

Father joins us at dinner. When Mother sits and I have poured tea for everyone, we all look at Father. He pulls an envelope from his pocket.

"A letter from Keiko," he says.

Mother reads the letter. She starts to speak, but then stops and hands the letter to Grandfather.

Grandfather waves his hand to Ron, and Mother gives the letter to Ron instead.

Ron scans the letter and looks up.

"Keiko writes that Professor Greene has held my place," Ron says.

I am glad Ron does not keep secrets like Mother and Father.

"He can try to get a pass for me to attend college again," Ron says.

Grandfather forms his hands into a steeple.

"You must go," Father says.

"Father," Ron says. "I will think about this. For you, I will think about this. And I will write to ask Professor Greene to tell me more about the pass. But I cannot promise to go. It is not my wish to leave my family in this place."

"You must!" Father says.

No one speaks for a few minutes. Then Father hits his palm against the table and stands. After another minute, he walks outside.

After Father leaves, we eat our dinner in silence. I am not hungry anymore, but it is easier to eat my food than to listen to Mother tell me why I must eat my food.

"What do you think, Mother?" Ron asks.

"I don't know what is right," Mother says. "The army, that was wrong. But college? That is not wrong. Only difficult."

"Difficult for me as well," Ron says. "To leave you in this place . . . I don't think I can do it."

"Children leave their parents, my son," Mother says.

Ron lowers his voice, but I lean closer to hear.

"But what about Manami?" he asks. "It isn't fair that

she must stay here and I can go. I don't think I can leave her either."

Mother looks at me.

"We will discuss this later," she says.

Ron turns toward me.

"You are a good listener, Little Sister, but sometimes you should not listen," he says. Then he squeezes my hand.

"It is time to walk home," Grandfather says.

That night, when I am in my bed, I remember that Ron did not mention Miss Rosalie's return. I wonder if he knows. It's hard for me to imagine that he doesn't. In this prison-village, everyone knows everything.

I walk to Miss Rosalie's classroom again the next day, this time with a newspaper flower. I saved it from the night of the lanterns. It is not colorful, but the petals curl under and swirl around each other. Miss Rosalie is outside, sweeping the steps.

"Oh, Manami!" she says when she sees me. "My darling girl!" She leans the broom against the building and hurries to meet me. "I'm teaching your class again. Isn't that the best news?"

I nod and hold my paper flower out to her.

Miss Rosalie brings the flower to her nose.

"It's so pretty, I can almost smell roses," she says. Then she puts her arm around my shoulders.

"Thank you for the beautiful painting," she says. "That was your painting, wasn't it? When I was here last, you only made drawings. Now paintings, too! And so beautiful!"

Miss Rosalie talks on and on. She doesn't wait for me to respond but just jumps from one subject to the next.

"I've made a new curtain," she says. "Just wait until you see it. I was tempted to make it white, but I chose light pink instead. I made a yellow one for your brother."

For the rest of the morning, I help Miss Rosalie clean desks and chairs. We hang the curtain, sweep the floor, and wash the window. By the time I leave to join Grandfather for lunch, Miss Rosalie's new classroom is sparkling.

"Come back tomorrow, if you can," Miss Rosalie says. "We can tackle your brother's classroom."

At dinner that evening Grandfather says, "School will start soon."

"We really don't have enough books still," Ron says. "But we will get by. I can organize my classroom this weekend so that I am ready when school begins on Monday."

"Manami has been helping her teacher today," Grandfather says.

Ron smiles. "I heard something about that," he says.

I think about the surprise Miss Rosalie and I have planned for him.

I can't wait for tomorrow.

The next morning, I watch as Mother takes out her teapot. I watch as she takes out a cup and a tray. I watch as she sets the teapot on the tray and the cup next to it.

"I thought you might like to take tea to your teacher," she says. She hands me the new tea tin left over from the lantern celebration, and I pour tea leaves into the teapot.

Together, Mother and I walk to the mess hall. She boils water and I pour it over the tea leaves. I carry the heavy tray to the school building and inside to Miss Rosalie's classroom. I set it down on her desk. Steam rises from the teapot as I pour a stream of tea into the cup.

She takes a sip and smiles. "Perfect," she says. Then she takes a cup from inside her desk and pours tea into it. She hands me the cup. We drink our tea in silence. Miss Rosalie smiles and looks out the window.

Ron's classroom is in the same block as Miss Rosalie's. It is not in the same barracks anymore, though. Now it is in the barracks next door. While we clean Ron's classroom, Miss Rosalie tells me about the new books she has brought:

two volumes of poetry. She tells me about the new box of paints she has brought: six different colors. She tells me about the calico kitten she has brought: Annabel Lee.

Miss Rosalie laughs when she tells me about her kitten. While she was staying with her aunt and uncle, the kitten appeared on their doorstep out of nowhere.

Like the dogs, I think.

"Of course I kept her," Miss Rosalie says. "Anyone would have kept her."

Loud clanging from the mess hall interrupts us.

"Hurry off to your lunch," Miss Rosalie says. "I'll finish up here. Your brother is going to be very surprised, don't you think?"

I look around Ron's classroom. It is neat and tidy, a curtain hanging over the window.

Maybe he will be surprised. Maybe he will be something else, too: maybe he will be happy.

Happy that I helped clean and organize his classroom.

Happy that Miss Rosalie made him a yellow curtain.

I put the cup and teapot on the tray and carry it to the mess hall.

After lunch, Mother tells me to rest.

Grandfather says that means I must take a nap.

But today I am not tired. So I lie on my bed with my paper and pencils.

Ron does not join us for dinner that evening. After we eat, Mother gives me a bowl of vegetables and noodles and chicken that is covered with a cloth.

"Perhaps he is working in his classroom," she says. "If he is not, set it on the table at home."

I take the bowl to Ron's classroom. On my way there, I see the wild boys playing baseball. They cackle and growl at each other, chasing around the diamond Ron made for them. Today there is a dog barking after them that is just as wild as they are.

I wonder where the dog came from.

I wonder what will happen to these wild boys if Ron returns to college. I wonder if their next teacher will buy them a bat, glove, and ball.

I wonder what will happen to me if Ron returns to college. I would miss him so much.

The door to Ron's classroom is closed but not pulled tight. I push it and it swings open without a sound.

I hear Ron's whisper voice but not his words.

I step into the doorway of Ron's classroom.

I look down. I do not want to interrupt.

"I cannot," Ron says.

His voice is sad. It is certain. It is a little bit angry.

I look up and my heart stops beating. It is my brother. His arms around Miss Rosalie. But not the same way he puts his arms around me. And Miss Rosalie's arms around Ron. But not the same way she puts her arms around me. Their heads tilt toward each other. Their faces shine damply in the dim light. I must make some kind of noise, because they both turn to me at the same moment.

My heart begins to beat again, and I feel shame stain my cheeks red. I wish I had run away before they saw me.

They jump apart, and then I look down. I do not want to see shame stain their cheeks red like mine.

I set the bowl of noodles and vegetables and chicken on the desk closest to me and turn to leave.

"Manami," Ron calls.

I do not want to hear what Ron wants to tell me. I do not want to be a good listener. So I walk out the door.

I start to run. I run past the wild boys. I run past the mess hall, where Mother is still cleaning.

When I reach the steps in front of our barracks I stop. I stand still until I feel so calm that Grandfather won't notice that I'm upset, and then I walk inside, past the table where he sits, to my bed, where I also sit.

Our room is the only place I can hide. Ron will not talk to me in front of the others.

I think about Ron and Miss Rosalie. Ron, who tells me secrets, but not this one. Miss Rosalie, who tells me stories, but not this one.

I wonder what other secrets I do not know.

Just before school starts, sickness begins to pass from one barracks to another.

"Rest," Mother tells me before she leaves for her shift at the mess hall.

"Eat," Father tells me before he leaves for his work crew.

But resting and eating don't help. I am too sick to start school with the other children.

Ron says nothing before he leaves for his classroom in the morning. But he pats my arm.

The sickness passing from barracks to barracks brings coughing and sneezing. It is mostly grandmothers and grandfathers who lie in bed. But what I feel is not in my lungs or in my nose. It is in my heart and my head. The sickness I feel has been growing larger and larger since I learned the secret between Ron and Miss Rosalie.

As the sickness grows larger, my throat shrinks smaller and smaller. Now not only do words not pass through my throat, but food cannot pass through either. Mother makes broth in the kitchen and Grandfather spoons it into my mouth.

Twice each day, I hear the chitter of my classmates as they walk to and from school. I wonder if the seat next to Kimmi is taken by someone new, or if the seat is waiting for me. I wonder if Miss Rosalie is waiting for me. When I think about Miss Rosalie, my stomach flips and my throat squeezes.

So I think of the dogs that now roam the paths of this prison-village.

I try to count them. One with Kimmi. One by the mess hall. Two with the cows. One with the wild boys. Perhaps even more have come since I've been sick.

I worry that other dogs will find the rest of the drawings. That there will be none left for Yujiin. How will he find me?

Mother and Father and Grandfather and Ron whisper when they think I am asleep.

"Something must be done," Father says.

"She is not getting better," Ron says.

"I think she is getting worse," Grandfather says.

"I will take her to the doctor," Mother says.

The next morning, Mother takes me to the hospital.

It is far away, as far away as it could be in this prison-village. It is behind Block 29, close to the cemetery.

A big truck stops at our barracks. Just like the day we left the island.

A soldier sits in the back with Mother and me. Just like the day we left the island.

The truck takes us to the hospital.

On the outside, the hospital looks like every other building here.

On the inside, it is wide open and filled with beds and curtains that separate the beds from one another.

Mother speaks to a nurse, and the nurse directs us to a bed.

I am tired from the trip, so I lie down.

The nurse pulls the curtain closed and checks me. Then the doctor checks me.

"I don't know what is wrong with her," the doctor says. "Maybe it is this harsh climate. Too hot. Too windy. Too dry. We can keep her here, if you need to work."

"I will take her home," Mother says.

I overhear Mother and Grandfather talk about me. They say words like *sorrow* and *heartsickness*. But I cannot tell them Ron's secret. I will not write it down.

One day after school, Mother brings Kimmi to my bed. Kimmi sits on a chair beside me.

"Can you sit up?" she asks. "I'll brush your hair."

Mother helps me sit and then leaves us alone.

While Kimmi brushes my hair, she tells me about school.

"Miss Rosalie and I are saving your seat," she says.

She tells me about her dog.

"Coco cries like a baby when my mother leaves her alone for two seconds," she says.

Then she sits on the other end of my bed, her legs crossed in front of her. She tells me rumors about the wild boys and complains about this morning's breakfast. She recites a poem she learned for school and whispers news of the war that sent us to this prison-village.

Mother brings us thinly sliced apples from the orchard. They smell so good. I pick one up and bite a tiny piece off. My throat has opened enough for me to swallow. And I am hungry for more apples.

Since I have been sick, my family is together again. Father does not spend his evenings with the other fathers. He spends them in our room with us. Ron does, too. I notice that they do not speak to each other. But at least they are in the same room.

During dinner, Mother must have told Father about Kimmi's visit that day. When he returns from the mess hall, he smooths my forehead with his big, rough hand.

"You ate some apples?" he asks. He is smiling.

Mother is in the mess hall, finishing her shift.

Father sits at the table, holding a block of wood and a knife.

Grandfather sits near the window, watching the night.

I hear a tapping at the door, and then Ron opens it and says, "I have brought Manami's teacher. She wishes to see Manami."

Father stands, placing the knife and wood on the table.

"Welcome," Father tells Miss Rosalie.

Father, Ron, and Miss Rosalie stare at each other.

At the same time, Grandfather stands and Mother returns.

"Mother, you remember Manami's teacher," Ron says.

"Welcome," Mother says. "You are kind to come."

"Thank you," says Miss Rosalie. "I have been worried about Manami."

I would like to close my eyes and pretend to sleep, but Ron saw that I was awake when he first entered.

I do not like to keep secrets like Father and Mother do.

Not even secrets for Ron, who does not keep secrets either. Especially not secrets from Mother, who makes me broth. Or Grandfather, who finds me paint. Or Father, who makes me a fan.

"Please sit," Mother tells Miss Rosalie.

Miss Rosalie sits. Ron sits. Grandfather sits. Father hovers. Mother brings a plate of crunchy cookies and pours glasses of water.

"Manami is sorry she has not returned to school," Grandfather says.

"I know she has been sick," Miss Rosalie says. "Many are sick now."

"With Manami, it is something different," Grandfather says.

"I see," says Miss Rosalie.

Ron and Miss Rosalie look at each other for a moment. From across the room, I can see that their secret will not stay a secret for much longer. Ron rises from his chair and stands behind Miss Rosalie. He puts his hands on her shoulders.

"I want you to know," Ron says. "Rosalie is more than just Manami's teacher."

For a moment, no one moves.

Then, Father huffs and leaves the room.

Mother closes her eyes and sets her glass on the table.

Grandfather leans back in his chair. But I cannot see his face.

"May I speak to Manami?" Miss Rosalie asks.

I close my eyes.

I hear a chair scrape across the floor.

"Hello, Manami," Miss Rosalie says.

I open my eyes. I do not want to, but I also do not want to hurt Miss Rosalie's feelings. But I cannot look at her, so I look at my hands instead.

"I have been worried about you," she says.

"The classroom feels empty without you," she says.

"My kitten is eager to meet you," she says.

"I have read nearly half of one of the new poetry books," she says.

"The walls of the classroom are covered with colorful paintings made by your classmates," she says.

Then she says nothing for a while.

I think she must be ready to leave, so I look up.

Miss Rosalie's face is close to mine. Our eyes meet.

"I miss you," she says. "Please come back."

I nod.

Miss Rosalie presses my hand and then stands.

• • •

The next morning, I return to school.

I walk with Ron.

He tells me about the new baseball team. It is a team full of wild boys.

He tells me about the student newspaper. His students are clever.

He tells me about Miss Rosalie's kitten, which escaped from its basket in her classroom and wandered all over her building.

Then he stops walking.

He crouches low to see my eyes, like Miss Rosalie.

"You love your teacher," he says. "You love Miss Rosalie. Perhaps you understand how I can love her, too."

And he is right. I can understand. I do understand. But I remember Father's words from last night.

"Forbidden," he said.

"Wrong," he said.

I remember Mother's words, too.

"Dangerous," she said.

"Impossible," she said.

I also remember Grandfather's words.

"Beautiful," he said.

"Love," he said.

This is the same word Ron says to me. Love.

"Can you understand how Miss Rosalie might love me, too?" Ron asks.

Yes. But: *Forbidden. Dangerous.* I understand these words, too, and I am afraid for my brother.

Kimmi is so happy to see me that she jumps up and down and squeals. She hugs me and spins me in a circle.

"You're back!"

Other children gather around. They smile and say hello. Even Ryo shouts, "Hey, Manami is back!"

When Miss Rosalie sees me in line during the pledge and song in the school yard, she hurries over. "Thank you for coming," she says.

Kimmi is behind me, Miss Rosalie is beside me, and Ron is across the way.

And I am happy to be at school.

OCTOBER

*E*very day, the air becomes a little bit colder and the days become shorter.

There are long shadows when I leave my classroom to walk home. The flagpole shadow spikes backward across the school yard. And the baseball diamond is dark before dinner.

Ron says the wild boys have not been in class for a few days. I would be happy about this except that Ron has been looking for them. I want Ron to stay far away from the wild boys who slink in shadows. I want the wild boys to stay far away from Ron.

On my way home, I see Ron under the long shadows talking to two wild boys he's caught.

I tiptoe closer.

I hear:

"What are you doing with this?" Ron asks, holding a paper.

"They are informers. Everyone on that list," a wild boy says.

"Passing along papers like this will get you into trouble,"

Ron says. "Let the men pass their own messages. You need to stay out of it."

"They spy," the other wild boy says. "Even on you! Then they tell the camp police."

"Come back to school," Ron says. "You want to get out of here? You need to be in school."

The wild boys leave, and Ron tears up the paper and puts the pieces in his pocket.

I do not move.

But Ron still sees me.

"Manami!" Ron says. His voice is angry and, I think, frightened. "Go home now!"

I run.

Mother's garden has dwindled to just three mounds of herbs. I help Mother cut the tops off the fruit and vegetable plants. Their stems are brown and the plants have stopped growing. All of the garlic and onions were dug up last month, and their dirt mounds are hard. Mother digs the dirt until it is soft and crumbly again. Then she pokes holes in it and shows me where to drop a tiny onion or garlic. These tiny onions and garlic are the ones she saved from the harvest. They will grow new onions and garlic for next year.

"They must freeze over the winter," Mother says. "Then they will grow strong for next summer."

We leave the herbs. If we don't trim them, they will make flowers. When the flowers grow as large as they can, Mother will cut them and collect their seeds.

When we are finished, Mother and I sit on the ground next to the herbs.

"This was a fine garden," Mother says. "Better than the island garden."

I look at Mother, and she must see my surprise. This garden grew tiny tomatoes and cucumbers. Mother's island garden grew large tomatoes and cucumbers.

"The island garden had plenty of rain," Mother says. "So much rain that it only grew shallow roots. This garden never had enough rain. So it had to grow deep roots. The island roots would never have survived the desert summer.

Mother takes the bowls I used every morning to water the garden and sets them next to my feet. She lifts my chin to look in my eyes. "You saved this garden, Daughter," she says. "Thank you."

Then she stands and returns to our room.

I'm not ready to go inside yet. I sit in the garden and look at what's left of it.

Mounds with onions and garlic buried inside, hibernating through winter's freeze.

Mounds with herbs at the end of their life cycle, growing flowers so that there will be herbs for next spring.

Mounds that sit empty, waiting for new seeds to grow new plants.

Strong plants.

Plants with deep roots.

Plants that survive.

One morning, Mr. Warden waits by the flagpole in the school yard. This is the first time I've seen him since I returned to school.

Today, he has brought camp police with him.

Mr. Warden and his policemen make me nervous.

When the students are lined up and waiting, he speaks.

"Salute! Pledge!"

My classmates' voices drone around me. When they stop, Mr. Warden walks up and down the lines of students.

"So many of you do not pledge," he thunders. "Why?"

My heart starts to pound and I wish I had stayed in bed.

Mr. Warden stops next to me.

"I remember you," he says. "You are the mute one."

Then he walks to another line. The wild boys.

"But you?" he says.

"And you?"

"And you?"

"And you?"

"You are not mute. So I ask again: Why do you not pledge?"

Ron steps forward.

"We will practice today," Ron says. "Tomorrow . . ."

Ron stops talking when Mr. Warden holds up his hand.

Mr. Warden motions to the camp police standing at the edge of the school yard. Their stomping boots make dust clouds as they walk toward us. Mr. Warden holds a paper up for Ron to see.

"I've seen these boys skulking in shadows."

He reads the paper. *"No freedom behind barbed wires."* He shakes the paper and looks at Ron.

"They are young," Ron says.

"Yes," Mr. Warden says. "They are young. But they are writing subversive tracts. And they are passing their subversive tracts around the camp for others to read. Do they write this with their teacher's guidance?"

Miss Rosalie puts her hand on her chest. But Ron is silent.

"Worse, there have been reports that they also act as messengers," Mr. Warden says. "They carry messages for some of the men about resistance and protest and violence."

Ron takes a step back. He looks at the wild boys. They do not look so bold anymore. Ron looks at me. Then he looks at Miss Rosalie.

"I know about the messages," he finally says. "I've tried to stop them."

Mr. Warden motions to the camp police again. "Bring him in for questioning." Then he leaves the school yard.

The policemen grab Ron's arms.

"I come willingly," Ron says.

The policemen release him and let him walk.

All I can think is that the camp police are taking Ron away. And something is wrong. But I do not understand what has happened.

"Take care of her!" Ron shouts over his shoulder.

Take care of her? Mother? Is that what he means?

I want to ask him what he means.

I want to ask him what is happening.

I want to ask him where he is going and when he will return.

But my throat is covered with dust.

I sway.

Miss Rosalie wraps her arms around me.

"Ron," she whispers.

Miss Rosalie stares at the wild boys.

"What have you done?" she says. "What have you done?"

Another teacher walks up the steps to the closest barracks and turns to face us. "No school today," he says.

I feel the eyes of the other students staring holes in my skin.

I stand in the school yard, my arms around Miss Rosalie, her tears wetting my hair, until we are the only two left.

Take care of her.

I will.

By evening, everyone in the prison-village knows what has happened.

In Block 3, they say Ron is honorable. He tried to help his students, the wild boys. But they would not be helped.

In other blocks, they say Ron is a traitor. He told Mr. Warden and his policemen the names of the men who send the wild boys to pass messages.

For now, Ron is in jail.

Father is allowed to see him for a moment. Long enough to be assured that Ron has not been harmed.

That night, Mother and Father and Grandfather sit around the table in our room. Like me, they do not speak. I wonder if dust has begun to coat their throats, too.

• • •

The day after Ron's arrest, rain comes. This rain pounds the remaining stalks and stems in Mother's garden into the hard ground.

"No matter," Mother says. "I have collected the flowers, and we have harvested all we can."

The rain brings thunder and lightning. Dogs cower under steps. Chickens squawk and flap inside their coops.

The rain churns the paths and roads of the prison-village into frothy puddles.

Mother and Grandfather both offer to walk to school with me the first day without Ron. But I do not want their company.

I get to the school yard and see that the students have already gone inside.

I take a deep breath of the rainy-wet air.

The rain has already started to flood the school yard, turning it into slick and sticky mud.

The mud makes the school yard look different.

It makes the school yard feel different.

It makes it easier for me to go to school without Ron.

Like it is a new place now. A place Ron never was.

I walk past Ron's empty classroom. His students now go to teachers in different barracks. It is temporary. Just until Ron comes back.

The students are quiet.

The teachers are quiet, too.

A worried kind of quiet. An afraid kind of quiet.

I stay after school to help sweep my classroom. Usually, Miss Rosalie chatters to fill up the empty space my throat leaves. She flits from one part of the classroom to another and shows me the curious things she's found around the school, like a heart-shaped rock or a tiny purple sage blossom.

But today she sits silently at her desk and stares out the window until I am done. Then she hands me paper and says, "Thank you, Manami. I'll see you tomorrow."

Already, I do not think I am doing a good job of taking care of Miss Rosalie.

NOVEMBER

When Father is home, he glowers. His anger blames the wild boys. It blames their fathers. It blames Mother and me. His anger blames Miss Rosalie.

Mother watches and waits. Her sorrow fills her eyes, brimming over when she thinks I am sleeping.

Grandfather's hands do not stop working. In his worry, he twists wires and sands wood pieces, making tiny boats and tiny houses.

Miss Rosalie's face grows more and more gaunt. Her grief causes shadows to ring her eyes.

Three days after Ron's arrest, the rain finally stops. No tapering off for this rain. One minute roaring and pounding, the next minute silence.

After dinner, I run to my classroom. The light is still on. I take Miss Rosalie's hand and bring her home with me. It is the only way I can think to take care of her.

At our small table, Mother feeds Miss Rosalie. Grandfather pats her arm. And, finally, Father speaks.

"He should have returned to Indiana," Father says.

"Yes," says Miss Rosalie.

"But he stayed here for you," Father says.

"Not for me," she says. "I begged him to go."

Mother whispers to Father.

He is still angry, but his voice is softer when he speaks again.

"You should be careful," he says.

"If you hear anything . . ." Mother says.

"I will tell you," Miss Rosalie says. "Thank you for welcoming me."

Mother grasps Miss Rosalie's hands. Then she motions to me to open the door.

I walk with Miss Rosalie through our block.

When we reach the administration buildings, Miss Rosalie stops.

"Thank you, my dear. Ron said . . ." Her voice breaks. "Ron said, 'Manami is the best little sister.' Hurry home."

I watch Miss Rosalie walk toward her home. When the darkness swallows her, I trudge through the mud to Block 3.

Just as our door closes behind me, I look in the direction of the school yard. In the faraway glow of a streetlight, I see the silhouette of a dog. It is hard to see clearly—the lamp is dim, the dog is far, our door closes quickly. But I think I see pointed ears. I think I see a small, firm body. I think I see a nose raised in the air. Has Yujiin finally come?

I push the door open again.

But the dog is gone.

I wonder where it has gone.

I wonder why I did not see it when I stood there with Miss Rosalie only minutes ago.

I take a step outside when something else catches my eye.

Gleaming white letters against black walls: *Watch out, traitors.*

The letters are so fresh that they drip.

I hurry back into our room, grab Grandfather's hand, and pull him with me. Father and Mother follow us.

When Father sees the letters, he says, "Go inside."

Mother and I wait in our room. After many minutes, Grandfather and Father return.

"It is gone," Father says. His sleeves are wet around his wrists and he has white smudges on his clothes. "I have to report this. But I want you to stay inside. From now on, none of you are to go out alone."

The next morning, Father doesn't go to work.

"We're going to visit Ron," he says.

When I don't move from the table right away, he picks up my coat and drapes it over my shoulders. "Come," he says.

Inside the jail, Ron sits at a table. Behind him, there are rooms with bars. As soon as we walk through the door, Ron stands.

"Father," Ron says in his whisper voice. He looks at the ground.

Mother hugs him. She reaches her hand up and smooths his hair back from his forehead. I do not hear what she says to him.

Grandfather hugs Ron next.

"Son," Father says. His voice rumbles.

Ron finally looks up.

"I'm sorry," Ron tells him.

"For leaving school?" Father asks.

"No," Ron says. "Not school. They told me about the words painted on the wall last night. I'm sorry for shaming you this way."

Father does not speak for a moment. Then he clears his throat. "This shame is not yours," he says.

A soldier comes inside the room with us. "Mr. and Mrs. Tanaka," he says. He looks at Grandfather.

"My grandfather," Ron says.

"Please sit," the soldier says. "We'd like to release Ron.

But even before the graffiti in your block last night, we knew it might not be safe for him. We can transfer him to another camp. Minidoka in Idaho seems like the best choice. But we can consider Arizona, too."

"Idaho? Arizona?" Mother whispers. "They are so far away."

"Or we can release him here," the soldier says. "But we can't guarantee his safety."

"What about at the other camps?" Father asks. "Can you guarantee his safety there?"

"No," the soldier says. "But I think it would be better than here."

"Can he return to school?" Grandfather asks.

"That might be an option down the road," the soldier says. "But there's a lot of paperwork to handle before that can happen, and we can't keep him in jail that long. I'll leave you folks to talk about it."

After the soldier is gone, Father speaks. "You must go," he says. "The soldier is right. It is not safe for you here."

"I agree," says Mother.

"Grandfather?" Ron asks.

"I think the only choice is which camp," Grandfather says.

Ron's shoulders slump.

"The camp in Idaho is closest to home," Mother says.

"Maybe it will be a place where you can come, too," Ron says.

By the time the soldier returns, Ron has told Mother what he would like her to pack for him.

"Have you made a decision?" the soldier asks.

"Minidoka," Ron says.

"I'll arrange for you to leave tomorrow," the soldier says.

Mother and Grandfather and Father wait at the door when Ron bends down next to me.

"I'm sorry I can't stay," he says.

I wrap my arms around his neck.

"Maybe this time you will come to me," Ron says.

I do not want to let go of Ron's neck, but Father picks me up and carries me.

I have so many tears that Father's shirt is wet when I rest my cheek against it.

Mother does not make me go to school after we leave the jail. She keeps me inside our room, folding sheets and blankets and clean clothes for Ron. She shows me where to stack Ron's books so that she can choose which to send with him. But when she is ready to pack his suitcase, she sends me outside.

"I need to concentrate," she says, "so I can get this done quickly before I have to go to work."

While I squat next to the empty mounds of Mother's garden, I can feel eyes staring at my back.

I spin around.

No one is there.

I can hear panting behind me.

I turn as fast as I can.

No one is there. Not anywhere.

I creep along the path as slow as I can. In case I feel something. In case I hear something.

But I don't.

Then a light breeze wafts past my nose. Salty, sandy, fresh.

I run. Back to where I saw the silhouette last night. Over to the water pump, where I remember shadows and whines. I look under steps, behind barracks, inside windows. I look and I run.

I run until Grandfather catches me.

He lifts me high into his arms, tight against his chest. He carries me home.

"He is not here, little one," Grandfather says.

I want to tell Grandfather he is wrong. I felt him. I heard him. I smelled him.

But I know Grandfather is right.

"He is not coming," Grandfather says.

I want to tell Grandfather he is wrong about that, too. The wind carried thirty-one drawings. And a message shone in my lantern.

But I know Grandfather is right.

Yujiin did not find my drawings. He did not see my message.

"You must stop looking for him," Grandfather says.

How can I stop looking for him?

I want to tell Grandfather: Remember? Once, I let him go. I let him go. *I.*

I wish dust would fill my nose so that I cannot smell. I wish dust would blow past my ears on the wind so that I cannot hear. I wish dust would cover my eyes so that I cannot see.

But mostly I wish I would not feel this big empty space inside of me. Yujiin is gone. And now Ron is gone, too.

When I am in bed that night, I overhear Grandfather's rumbling low voice.

"Perhaps enough time has passed that Manami is ready for a dog now," he says.

"Do you think she has forgotten Yujiin?" Father asks. "Then why isn't she talking?"

"She will not forget Yujiin," Grandfather says. "But Manami is the kind of girl who must have something to care for. Caring for the garden was good for her. And I think her heart is ready for a new friend. Especially now that Ron is leaving. Maybe her new friend will teach her to talk again."

After a while, Father says, "I will ask the soldiers if there are any new dogs."

The room becomes silent after their talk. Then I hear sleeping sounds: soft breaths, light snores. Is Grandfather right? Will a new friend fill the empty space inside of me? Will a new friend help me talk again? It takes a long time for me to fall asleep.

The next morning, Mother says, "I will walk to school with you."

We leave early. Mother doesn't want to meet anyone on the way, I think. She carries a bowl with a cloth wrapped around it.

Mother motions for me to wait outside when she walks up the steps to Miss Rosalie's classroom. But I pretend I don't see her and follow behind.

Tears slide down Mother's cheeks when she tells Miss Rosalie, "We saw him yesterday. He has gone to Minidoka in Idaho, where he will be safe. Safer than here."

"If only he had returned to Indiana," Miss Rosalie says.

"If he had returned to Indiana, then he would be someone else," Mother says.

Mother puts her arms around Miss Rosalie, hugging her close.

She puts the bowl filled with salty-sour rice balls in Miss Rosalie's hand.

Mother is taking care of Miss Rosalie, too.

Later, in class, Miss Rosalie tells us stories about her kitten. It is not chatter, but it is not silence either.

She walks around the room, touching each student's shoulder. It is not flitting, but it is not sitting either.

When I walk home, I wrap my scarf around my head, covering my ears. I hold my hands alongside my eyes, blocking everything except what is right in front of me. This way I cannot listen or look.

I think I will make an ocean picture in the dirt. In Block 3. In front of our barracks.

I unwrap my scarf and hand it to Grandfather.

First, I sweep the dirt in front of our barracks. The mud is gone and the dirt is hard, so it is easy to sweep it smooth.

Next, I use Grandfather's rake to draw waves in the dirt. I have to dig into it to carve out the waves and show their curling edges.

I add a beach and my sitting rock.

Grandfather sits on the steps in front of our room and looks at the ocean waves.

"Listen to the waves roll in and out," Grandfather says. "Watch them. Breathe in and out with them."

The waves reach beyond the prison-village. Beyond the mainland. All the way to the island.

I breathe in and out.

And suddenly, I hear a yap.

I see a fluffy little body run across the waves and along the beach.

I hear Grandfather take in a quick breath.

I see Father and Mother coming toward me.

I jump up and run.

For a second I think, Yujiin!

Only, now that I hold him in my arms, I see that it is not Yujiin. He is white, like Yujiin. Fluffy, like Yujiin. Soft, like Yujiin.

He puts his nose in my neck, like Yujiin.

He licks my chin, like Yujiin.

Father speaks. "A soldier said someone abandoned this dog by the gate. It's been following him around, but he does not want it."

Mother speaks. "He is not Yujiin. But he is yours, if you will have him. He needs someone to take care of him."

Grandfather speaks. "He will not replace Yujiin in your heart. But he will make your heart bigger to fit himself inside, too."

I take this fluffy white dog—who is not Yujiin and will not replace Yujiin—inside the house. I pour water from a pitcher into a small bowl and set it on the floor. I break a hard cookie into pieces, put the pieces in a small bowl, and set the bowl next to the water. After he eats and drinks, I make a nest for him on my bed. I curl up beside him, tucking him into my arms. He snorts and sighs and sleeps. Grandfather was right. I have taken care of him. And I feel my heart growing bigger.

DECEMBER

*A*s hot as the summer was in this prison-village, winter is that cold. Winter is not wet, like on the island. It is dry. Cold and dry.

Sores stretching across my chapped knuckles rip open and bleed. Skin peels from my lips. My eyes sting and burn.

At least there is no fresh dust to coat my nose and mouth. At least there is a soft body to warm me at night.

Father calls my small friend Seal.

"Dark eyes, dark nose," Father says. "White, just like a seal pup."

Seal and Grandfather walk me to school in the morning. They sit on the steps of our barracks during the day, having long conversations, which are just between themselves, Grandfather says. They meet me near the flagpole in the school yard at the end of the day.

During school hours, Seal is sometimes Grandfather's dog, resting by his side. He is sometimes Father's dog, trotting around the work crew. He is sometimes Mother's dog, waiting at the door of the mess hall.

But in the hours before school and after school, Seal is my dog. He bounces and yaps at me even though I cannot laugh. He whines and follows me even though I cannot call. And when his body is pressed close to my chest, or when he wags his tail while he laps up potatoes and chicken, or when he flops onto the steps watching the path, my heart squeezes closed.

It should be Yujiin who bounces and yaps.

It should be Yujiin who whines and follows.

It should be Yujiin who wags and flops.

My heart hurts and I remember that it is my fault that Yujiin is wandering alone out there.

Then Seal rests his nose on my neck and my heart opens up again.

But even with Seal pressed against me, I am not happy.

Not happy in this prison-village.

Not happy without Ron.

When I watch Father and Mother, it is not unhappiness I see. It is fear.

Fear on the faces of many in Block 3. The air hums with the stomping boots of soldiers and policemen.

Until one night, I hear sirens and screams.

The next morning we hear the news:

A man was beaten.

By men wearing masks.

By men who, under those masks, have faces just like mine.

I remember the wild boys and their talk of spies and traitors.

I am glad that Ron has gone away.

Fear swells all day. A few people gather by the administration buildings. Then a few more and a few more. The crowd grows until it is bigger than all of the people in Block 3. More people than many blocks combined.

Fear grows from a hum to crackles and sizzles. Softly at first, then louder and louder.

"Riot! Stay inside!" is whispered from barracks to barracks in Block 3.

But even inside, I can hear crackles and sizzles turn into roars.

Shouts.

Shots.

The next day, we hear whispers:

Two boys shot.

One is dying.

One is dead.

After the riot, school is canceled.

Kimmi and Coco stay in our room while Kimmi's mother works. Kimmi tries to teach Seal to balance a paper ball on his nose.

No one goes out alone.

No one goes out for long.

We receive a letter from Ron.

It is creased and a little dirty.

Mother passes the note to me to read.

Minidoka is cold, even colder than where we are now. Otherwise, it looks the same. Blocks of barracks. Endless space, but no ocean. There is snow already. This camp just opened. It is not full yet. It has few families and few children. The people who are in the camp are from Washington and Oregon.

When Father comes home, Mother hands Ron's letter to him.

"There are few families there," Grandfather says. "But there are families."

"There are few children there," Grandfather says. "But there are children."

"Shall we try to go there?" Mother asks.

"Yes," Father says.

"Yes," Grandfather says.

Yes, I think.

A week after the riot, the prison-village starts to return to normal.

That morning, Mother puts a note in my hand for Miss Rosalie.

Even though school hasn't started again, I find Miss Rosalie in her classroom.

"Yes!" Miss Rosalie says, after reading the note. "This is what I was thinking, too!"

I can guess what Mother wrote: We will try to go to Ron.

Grandfather and Seal are waiting for me outside. On our way home we run into Kimmi.

"Hello, Mr. Ishii," she says. She drops onto the ground next to Seal and scratches his ears.

We follow Grandfather, and Kimmi swings my hand as we walk. Seal runs back and forth between us and Grandfather.

"Just like the island," Kimmi says.

That evening, all of the island fathers from Block 3 meet after dinner in the mess hall. Grandfather goes, too.

When they return to our room, Father tells Mother what happened.

Many in Block 3 are unhappy. The beating, the riot, the violence.

Many in Block 3 want to leave this place. They have letters from friends who were sent to Minidoka, Ron's camp.

There is a new warden at our camp. Maybe he will listen.

Father will request a meeting with him. He will ask him if our family can be moved to join Ron at Minidoka. He will ask him if all of the Block 3 families can go to Minidoka.

Mother writes a letter to Keiko.

I draw a picture of Yujiin.

"Perhaps there is a way to send Manami to Keiko," Father says.

"No, it is not possible," Mother says. "She is too young."

The next morning, Father leaves earlier than usual. He carries with him the letter to be sent to Keiko.

Father returns that evening with a glum face.

"I wasn't able to schedule a meeting with the warden," he says.

Father tries again the next day.

And the next.

On the fourth day, Father returns to Block 3 with a smile.

"There must be good news," Grandfather says to me when he sees Father's smile.

Father tells us the warden will make arrangements for all of the island families in Block 3 who wish to move to the new camp.

There will be a meeting tonight to discuss the details.

It will take time for the new camp to be ready for so many people.

The warden said that not everyone will move at the same time.

But everyone should be moved by the end of January.

Mother and Father attend the meeting, but Grandfather and I wait in our room. Grandfather carves a block of wood. I brush Seal's short, thick fur.

"The first transport leaves in two weeks," Father says when he and Mother come home.

I pick up Seal. Will we have to leave him behind?

Mother puts her arm around me and whispers in my ear. "We will hope," she says.

Mother sends me with another note for Miss Rosalie.

When I find her in her classroom she says, "It's funny

to be in class without students, but I don't know what else to do."

I hand her the note.

"You are really leaving," Miss Rosalie says after she reads it. Her eyes are bright and I think she is going to cry.

I touch her hand.

"It's all right," she says. "I want you to go so that Ron is not alone. But I will miss you."

She takes her hand from mine and hugs me. "It's for the best," she whispers.

I look around the classroom trying to memorize everything about it.

The pink curtain.

Miss Rosalie's desk, with its collection of pretty things she found. Rocks, seeds, a nest.

Pictures drawn by me and my classmates tacked to the walls. Sailboats, cities, faces.

A square room with four walls.

Her books on a shelf.

When I go home, I start to draw a picture of Miss Rosalie on a piece of paper. It takes a few days before it is right. I want this picture to be perfect. I want to give this picture to Ron.

• • •

When she is not working, Mother sorts and folds and packs our suitcases. Kimonos, dresses, pants, shoes, Father's tools. She wraps the seeds she saved from the last harvest, and she washes blankets and sheets. Mother digs into the hard, frozen earth of her garden for tiny onions and garlic. She breaks dirt with a hammer until it is crumbly and fills a pillowcase. She stuffs her onions and garlic into the dirt sack and wraps it in a sheet.

Mother writes letters to Keiko and Ron.

I would like to help Mother pack, but she sends me outside to play with Seal.

The day before we leave, Mother keeps me home. All morning, I help her clean our room.

After lunch, Grandfather says, "Walk with me."

We walk past our barracks and past Block 1 and Block 2, Seal skipping between our legs. We walk along the fence. We walk until we reach a shrunken puddle of icy mud.

Grandfather unlaces his shoes and steps out of them. He peels off his socks and puts them in his shoes. He steps into the mud.

"Come," Grandfather says. His smile is wide.

The icy mud is colder than I imagined. It is so cold that I worry whether my toes might freeze and fall off my feet.

"If you close your eyes, you can almost hear ocean waves," Grandfather says. "Rolling in, rolling out."

"You can almost smell ocean salt," Grandfather says. "Tangy, sharp."

"You can almost feel ocean breeze," Grandfather says. "Cool, moist."

I close my eyes and listen and smell and feel. Grandfather is right. My breath rolls in and out like the ocean waves. I feel calm spread from my chest to my head and arms and legs.

When I open my eyes, Grandfather is smiling at me.

"You see?" he asks.

I use Grandfather's handkerchief to wipe and dry my feet before I put my shoes back on.

Together, we walk through the prison-village that has become our home. We stop at the water pump, the mess hall, Mother's garden. When we reach my classroom, I want to see if Miss Rosalie is there so I can say goodbye to her. Grandfather walks home, Seal in his arms.

Miss Rosalie sits at her desk, a pen in her hand and a book in front of her. But she is looking out the window.

When she notices me, she stares for several silent seconds. Then she stands.

"I heard you are leaving tomorrow," she says. "I was hoping you would come to say goodbye."

I run to Miss Rosalie and wrap my arms around her waist. She drops to her knees and hugs me back.

"I am glad," Miss Rosalie says. "I am glad. But I am also sad."

The layers of dust coating my throat begin to crack as tears wash my cheeks.

"This will not last forever," Miss Rosalie says. "It cannot."

Miss Rosalie releases me to get something from her desk. She walks me to the classroom door and puts a book in my hand. "For Ron," she says. "He likes these poems." Then she takes the scarf from her neck and ties it around mine. "For you," she says. Then she gives me a stack of paper.

"The address of my uncle and aunt is on the top paper. I do not know how much longer I will stay here, but you can always reach me through them," Miss Rosalie says. "Now, dry your eyes. You are brave, Manami. You are strong."

Then she kisses my forehead.

"I love you," she says.

I dry my eyes and walk home, my throat aching from the widening cracks.

Seal sits on the steps of our barracks while Grandfather wipes him with a cloth.

"He should be clean when we reach our new home," Grandfather says.

• • •

That evening, Father and Grandfather and I walk to the mess hall. Normal and not normal.

I pour steaming tea into four cups. Normal and not normal.

We sit on a bench while we wait for Mother to finish her shift so that we can all walk home together. Normal and not normal.

Normal would be: Grandfather and me walking into the mess hall alone and Father joining us later.

Normal would be: pouring steaming tea into five cups.

Normal would be: walking home without Mother and waiting for her there while she finishes her shift.

Before we leave the mess hall, Kimmi squeezes onto the bench beside me.

"I will miss you," she whispers into my ear.

I put my arms around her and hug her tightly.

"Save a seat for me in the new school," she says before she runs back to sit with her mother.

We hear whispers from our island neighbors as we walk through Block 3 to our barracks.

"We will join you soon," our neighbors say.

"Find a good spot for a garden," our neighbors say.

"Travel safely," our neighbors say.

We do not say goodbye to the other families.

Mother does not lay out our best clothes for tomorrow.

"Sleep," she says, and sends me to bed.

Seal jumps onto my bed and curls into a ball.

His black nose and black eyes remind me of Yujiin's.

Remind me of the island.

Of leaving the island and coming here.

Of leaving Yujiin.

I snuggle deep under the blanket with Seal in my arms. The cold day has turned into an even colder night.

I think of Mother's words.

We will hope.

In the morning, four suitcases line up in our room.

Dark clouds cover the sun, cover the sky. Dark and heavy and low.

I button Seal inside my coat and drag my suitcase, following Father and Mother and Grandfather down the dirt road to the gate.

We wait while our suitcases are loaded in the bottom of the bus.

We wait with the other families who are on the first bus to Minidoka.

The dark and heavy clouds look ready to burst.

No one speaks.

The door to the bus opens and we start to board.

Just when it is our turn, Seal pops his head out the neck hole of my coat to lick my chin.

"Stop!" says the soldier standing beside the bus door. "No dogs allowed."

Father freezes, one foot on the bus step, one foot on the ground.

Mother reaches toward me.

Grandfather hunches over.

I unbutton my coat and hold Seal's nose close to mine. He smells of sage and dust. He licks at the tears on my cheeks. I pull him close to my body and our hearts beat against each other.

The cracks in my throat rip wide open.

I remember Miss Rosalie's words: I am brave. I am strong.

"No!" I say. "No!"

I push past Grandfather and Mother and Father. I stand before the soldier who will drive the bus.

"No!"

All of the words I couldn't say are buried deep inside the one word I can speak.

The driver looks at my face. He looks at Seal licking my tears. He waves us on.

I keep walking, past other families, all the way to the back of the bus. I sit on the long seat under the long window. I button Seal's warm body inside my coat and watch as the heavy, dark clouds finally burst.

White flakes swirl, blowing past the window.

Snow.

The bus roars and pulls away from the gate.

Behind me, I see the prison-village waking up. My classmates walking to the mess hall. Fathers and mothers on their way to work. Dogs running, walking, sitting, waiting.

I see sharp barbed-wire fences.

What is ahead of me, I cannot see. I know Ron is there. New classmates and fathers and mothers. New dogs and new fences.

Mother walks toward me, her hands grasping the seats as the bus drives to the highway. She is crying. Father and Grandfather are behind her. They are crying, too.

And they are laughing.

"Manami!" Father says.

Mother wraps her arms around me and Seal. "My sweet girl," she says.

Grandfather sits beside me and pats my leg.

"I love you," I say. It is a scratchy whisper in my dry throat. But I say it again, "I love you." Strong. Like me.

I practice using my voice.

"Seal," I say.

He pops his head out.

"Seal," I say.

His mouth opens wide, his tongue hanging off to the side. His ears perk and his eyes blink.

"Seal," I say. And I laugh.

My throat is open again. I can see and smell and hear.

I can speak.

Strong words.

Brave words.

AUTHOR'S NOTE

In the late 1800s, Japanese immigrants came to the United States in large numbers. Most of these immigrants settled in Hawaii, California, Oregon, and Washington. The first immigrants to arrive worked on sugarcane plantations and fruit and vegetable farms. But in the early 1900s, they started buying or leasing their own land.

Through hard work, Japanese American farmers built successful farms, and many non-Japanese farmers in California became angry. In 1913, the state passed a law prohibiting Japanese immigrants from buying land. Eleven years later, the United States passed the Immigration Act of 1924, which banned immigration from Japan.

The Japanese Americans living in the United States were caught between countries. For many of them, returning to Japan was not a possibility. And yet they were not fully welcome in the United States. Consequently, many did not integrate into American society and, instead, lived together in Japanese American communities, holding on to their traditions and culture. They built lives for themselves in their new country. They owned businesses and stores and operated large farms. They raised families, sent their children to college, and made plans for their future.

All of that changed on December 7, 1941, when Japan attacked U.S. warships at a navy base in Pearl Harbor, near Honolulu, Hawaii. After this attack, the United States officially entered World War II, fighting against Japan, Germany, and Italy.

For the next two months, Japanese Americans became targets of fear and suspicion. Newspapers published articles that questioned their loyalty. Community leaders were arrested.

Then, on February 19, 1942, President Franklin D. Roosevelt signed Executive Order 9066, declaring areas along the west coast of the United States military zones. In order to protect these zones from espionage, certain groups of people would not be allowed to live there. The document did not specifically single out Japanese immigrants and their children, but it gave the U.S. Army the freedom to determine who could live in a military zone and who could not. The army decided that Japanese Americans, along with their children who had been born in the United States and who were therefore U.S. citizens, had to leave these zones because they might be spies for Japan.

In March 1942, the U.S. Army's Western Defense Council asked them to move to other parts of the United States or to a relocation camp. Those who did not volunteer were evacuated by force. Most Japanese Americans had nowhere else to go—they didn't have enough time to find another place to live—and they didn't realize how long they would be gone. On March 24, 1942, the Japanese Americans living on Bainbridge Island were given just six days to relocate. They left the island on March 30, and arrived at Manzanar on April 1.

By September 1942, over 100,000 Japanese Americans had been moved to relocation camps. Of those, 70,000 were U.S. citizens and about half of those imprisoned were children. Those who chose military service were allowed to leave the camp. In fact, many of the 30,000 Japanese Americans serving in the U.S. Armed Forces during World War II had family members living in relocation camps.

The relocation camps were in remote areas, surrounded by fences and guarded by soldiers with machine guns. There were ten in all: Heart Mountain in Wyoming, Tule Lake and Manzanar in California, Topaz in Utah, Poston and Gila River in Arizona, Amache in Colorado, Minidoka in Idaho, and Jerome and Rowher in Arkansas.

Few of the Japanese Americans in relocation camps were ever charged with crimes. And none were charged with espionage. Nonetheless, they lost their homes, their businesses, and their communities. Many were separated from family members.

Most of the incarcerees at Manzanar came from cities in California. They were used to a way of life different from that of the Bainbridge Islanders, who came from a rural community. Because of these differences, there were tensions between the two groups. On December 5 and 6, 1942, thousands of prisoners at Manzanar rioted. During this riot, a seventeen-year-old boy and a twenty-one-year-old man were shot. The boy died instantly. The man died a few days later. The Bainbridge Island families asked to be moved to Minidoka in Idaho, where Japanese Americans from Washington and Oregon were imprisoned. By early 1943, any Bainbridge Island families who wanted to move to Minidoka were given permission to go.

The war ended in 1945, three years after the first relocation camp was opened. Japanese Americans were allowed to leave the camps and given train tickets. But many no longer had homes to return to and now had to start over with few belongings.

In 1988, the U.S. Congress passed Public Law 100-383, an official apology to Japanese Americans for their treatment during World War II. It had taken more than forty years, but finally the government admitted its grave injustice. The apology applied both to survivors and to their family members.

Almost fifty years after the last Japanese American prisoner left, Manzanar was reopened as a National Historic Site. Today, visitors can walk the grounds, look at photos, and read first-person accounts of those who lived there. Many of the relocation camps were torn down, but according to the National Park Service, the mission of the site is "to serve as a reminder to this and future generations of the fragility of American civil liberties."

A final note about the lantern festival: Obon is a summer festival celebrated in Japan to honor one's ancestors. The lantern festival described in this book is a version of Obon, and although it didn't actually happen at Manzanar in the summer of 1942, versions of Obon and other holidays, both Japanese and American, were celebrated at different camps throughout the war.

RESOURCES

Bainbridge Island Japanese American Community: "BIJAC." http://www.bijac.org/.

Densho: The Japanese American Legacy Project. Digital archive of video oral histories of Japanese Americans incarcerated or interned during World War II. http://www.densho.org/.

Lindquist, Heather C. *Children of Manzanar*. Berkeley, Calif.: Heyday Books, 2012.

National Park Service. "Manzanar National Historic Site." http://www.nps.gov/museum/exhibits/manz/index.html.

Unrau, Harlan D. *The Evacuation and Relocation of Persons of Japanese Ancestry During World War II: A Historical Study of the Manzanar War Relocation Center*. United States Department of the Interior, National Park Service, 1996.

ACKNOWLEDGMENTS

My first thanks to my friend Stephanie Shaw for being the first person to read *Paper Wishes*. Many thanks to the lovely ladies of Crumpled Paper—Lisa Robinson, Maria Gianferrari, Sheri Dillard, Andrea Wang, and Abby Aguirre—whose fingerprints are all over this story. And a big thank-you to my friend Jamie Weil for so many late-night phone calls.

My gratitude to Margaret Ferguson and Kathleen Rushall for loving Manami and Yujiin as much as I do. And endless thanks to my family—Amir, Bella, and Julian—for making space for me to write.